Boston Boomer Boy –

A Childhood Memoir

By

John Staniland

Also by the Author

Life with the Lions – Rugby and travel adventures in Australia

following the British and Irish Lions tour of 2001

Following the Rising Sons – Rugby and travel adventures in

South America and Japan following the progress of the England

Rugby Team

Midlife Meanderings in S E Asia – An account of an ageing

traveller's budget journeys through S E Asia

Searching for My Shangri La – More stories of random

travelling in Asia

For more information and travel blogs visit

www.johnstanilandtravelwriter.com

To Cam

CHAPTER 1

EARLY RECOLLECTIONS

I was flicking through the Sunday Times literary section when I came across a review of *On Chapel Sands* by Laura Cumming. The reviewer highly recommended the book as a memoir and a mystery tale, and it would become a huge bestseller. But I was interested to read further to establish whether the 'Chapel Sands' in question were my Chapel Sands or not. It delighted me to confirm that the author had primarily set the book in a small village on the East Coast.

Shortly after World War 2, two of Dad's brothers built wooden holiday bungalows on the Lincolnshire coast. The location was just a few miles up from Billy Butlin's first holiday camp and the traditional seaside resort of Skegness. The bungalows were at a caravan and chalet park, close to the village, or perhaps more accurately the tiny hamlet, of Chapel St. Leonards. This was just a few yards to the west of the dunes and the vast expanses of beautifully sandy but often windswept North Sea beaches.

The local authority had divided the beach up by using wooden groynes running out to sea every two hundred yards. They had put these in place to reduce the erosional impact of the mighty North Sea waves. Further along, to the north, were vast concrete sea walls to keep the ocean at bay.

This unprepossessing place played an essential part in my growing up.

It was also conveniently only some 20-odd miles from the town of Boston where we all lived. Boston was a market town, set in the middle of a highly fertile arable area, focussing on the production of potatoes, sugar beet, cabbages and cauliflowers. It was also a fishing and commercial port. In those days, the population was around 25,000 people.

The home fleet of fishing smacks, which were berthed in the tidal River Haven, known as the River Witham beyond the Sluice Bridge, used to motor out on the tide. They would chug out in a long convoy to the prolific fishing grounds of the Wash.

Timber and general cargo vessels used the commercial docks. They came from countries directly over the other side of the North Sea, the Baltic nations, and even Russia. The ships reached Boston's port facilities via a separate channel a couple of miles up the River Haven towards the sea.

Summer weekends and school holidays, a boisterous crowd of siblings, cousins, aunts, uncles and friends (many from the Boston Swimming Club or Boston Rugby Club where Dad and Uncle David were leading lights) disgorged to Chapel for simple fun times at the seaside.

We would trek up and down the sand hills in warm summer weather, taking various curving paths through the dense, spiky tufts of marram grass. Different group members would carry all the bats and balls, buckets and spades and other holiday paraphernalia, deckchairs, and picnic baskets and set up camp for the day. Two of the men would lug a giant orange eight-man inflatable boat liberated from the RAF at some stage just after the war. The life raft was great fun to take out into the crashing, grey, white-flecked breakers. Being almost impossible to control, this resulted in multiple capsizes, lots of laughter and general hilarity.

A few years ago, my mum, when we were reminiscing about childhood holidays, blabbered something, after she had enjoyed a couple of glasses of wine. She told me my conception had occurred in the sand hills at Chapel St. Leonards. Hopefully, somewhere away from the primary routes, and other holidaymakers. My April birthday would show that I probably had resulted from some summer frolics in the dunes. No wonder this bleakly beautiful and almost lonely stretch of sand and dunes meant so much to me.

I have some vivid memories of my early childhood in Boston, going back to when I was only around three or four years old,1953. One time which particularly resonated, because I remember being so scared, was when I was with Mum very late one winter's night. She had kept me up well beyond my usual bedtime to give her some needed company.

Mum and I were very close. I was her firstborn, and she was only twenty-two when I arrived on the scene, so I think I was very special to her. She later told me she always wanted a boy, but if that had not been the case, I would have been called Jane Elizabeth rather than John Edward.

Very late into the night, Dad and several uncles and friends returned to our house on Station Street exhausted, wet, bedraggled and deeply saddened by their experiences of the day. I was too young to understand what had been happening entirely, but I could readily see, even at my tender age, that they had all endured a traumatic ordeal. Their grey and drawn faces and their soft, sad voices showed something of what they had been through that long winter's day and night.

On the evening of the 31st January 1953, the Spring tides, an intense low-pressure weather system, and a howling northerly gale combined to devastating effect to cause the North Sea to breach the dunes and artificial seawalls and smash down the defensive groynes set all along the Lincolnshire coast. Forty-three people in Lincolnshire alone lost their lives. Further afield, the floods caused even more significant damage in Norfolk and on the other side of the North Sea in Holland and Belgium. The overall death toll from the storms and the resultant floods was significantly higher, estimated at over two and a half thousand.

Once they had heard of the disaster early in the morning, the men in the family rallied around and got to Chapel St. Leonards as soon as they could to help in whatever way possible. The storms and raging seas had decimated their holiday chalets. They would need to be rebuilt from scratch. But the freak conditions had rendered many people injured or homeless, and looking after their requirements became the priority.

Catastrophic flooding occurred. Its extent was immense, covering scores of square miles. Topographically, the area was essentially like a billiard table. Dutch engineers some 200 years previously had reclaimed much of the land from the sea, but it was very flat and low-lying, so susceptible to flooding.

The storms meant that as well as lives being lost and properties being destroyed and flooded, saltwater rendered many thousands of acres of valuable and rich agricultural land useless. It was a major disaster.

15A Station Street, Boston, was a corner shop and a house; Dad thought that as Mum had to give up her post office job to look after me, she could also manage a fruit and vegetable and small grocery store. He presumably thought this was an effective way to supplement the family income. The spacious Victorian property was our first family home, although Mum and Dad had started their married life 'in rooms' as they described it before having me. I enjoyed the benefits of being an only child here for three years until my middle brother, Robert, came along.

I think Mum enjoyed the time when it was just me and her. She had her little boy, just like she had always wanted, and we forged an unbreakable bond.

When I was just a toddler, I remember Dad fractured his skull in a stupid accident. When standing astride his bicycle, chatting to two young nurses he knew, on the quayside above Boston's tidal River Haven, he slipped and fell. He went headlong into the thick, black, sticky mud some fifteen feet below. His head struck the unforgiving steel hull of a fishing smack on the way down. After his recovery in Boston hospital, they sent him to see a specialist in Sheffield to find out if there had been any long-term damage to his faculties.

"Where has Daddy gone?" I remember I asked Mum one day, and she explained where he was and that he would come home soon on the train.

It was all I needed to know as we lived close to the railway terminus, as our street name would suggest. I snuck out and toddled off to the station to meet my dad. I got onto the platforms where the loud screeches and squeals coming from the enormous black locomotives and the regular hissing and belching of steam and smoke were both fascinating and frightening. The taste of soot was on my tongue, and I could smell the pungent fumes and feel the vibrations as the vast engines moved off. The sight of crowds of bustling adults rushing to and from the trains and loudly slamming the carriage doors was also disturbing. I looked around in awe, a certain fear, and wonderment when Mum suddenly arrived and swept me up into her arms. She appeared upset, but I did not know why. I was only looking for Daddy.

I clearly remembered another occasion when I gave my mum the willies - I was a little mischievous. One day, a lady came into the shop and, in a panicked voice, screamed,

"Here, missus, your little boy is outside your bedroom window!"

Indeed, being adventurous and wanting to explore my surroundings, I opened a bedroom window and got out onto the tiny balcony protected only by foot-high ornamental cast-iron railings.

Over the road from the shop, there lived a large family who seemed to be very poor, even to a little boy of my age, with innumerable children running around in rags and mostly shoeless. They were the Brewsters, and the man of the house was a fisherman. His income depended on the catch's size, and often when the Wash was reluctant to release her bounty, or the weather was too rough to venture out, they barely had a couple of pennies to rub together.

Mum, out of kindness, used to let them run a tab at the shop until their finances improved, which they did after a good haul of fish. They then cleared the debt and old man Brewster would often give us a bonus of a sizeable fresh lobster. I used to enjoy the lobster treat, and it must have been the start of my gaining a sophisticated palate and an appreciation of gourmet food.

Mum also used to help Mrs Brewster with Friday night bath time when they lined all the little ones up by the fire in the scullery. They had to take their turn in the tin bath and wallow in a few inches of tepid grey water. There were eleven kids, but poor Mrs Brewster was to die trying to give birth to number twelve.

***

Fast forward some 60 years, and I phoned my brother, who was a few miles ahead of us in Boston. He was driving Dad on a sentimental trip to his hometown, not long after Mum had passed away. I was following in my car with my daughter and we were trying to meet up.

"Where are you?"

"On the Haven quayside looking over to the Baths," Rich replies.

"Yes, I know exactly where you mean. We'll be there in ten minutes."

We pulled up, and I could see them, chatting to an old fishing chap in a denim cap and a thick navy blue woollen jumper on the dock. As they were deep in conversation, we just nodded our presence.

Dad was explaining to the man that when he was much younger, he occasionally went out on a fishing smack called the Drummer Boy owned by his sister's father-in-law, old man Yarnold. Dad was not an accomplished sailor and ended up spending a lot of time being sick over the rail. But he reckoned he enjoyed the long days of camaraderie and physical work out on the waters of the Wash. Sustained only by thick, black, sweet tea constantly stewing on the pot-bellied stove, he endured long hours from pre-dawn until after dusk doing backbreaking work. Just for fun.

The man interrupted him.

"She went down in '69, the Drummer Boy. A freak accident in perfect weather, ploughed into by The Telegraph. Went down in two minutes, they reckoned, but they saved everyone."

We contemplated this for a moment, and then the conversation moved on.

"This is my boat," he said, pointing to the empty, tidy-looking vessel, whiffing of fishy remnants below us in the low water.

"And the two along there are my boys. Cockles mainly. Fished all my life I have."

All three boats appeared modern, and the sons' boats moored just a few yards up the river, close to a newish cockle landing wharf, looked to be in perfect nick.

We looked across the Haven to an old Victorian building on the opposite shore, the Municipal Swimming Baths. This humble but handsome grey brick-built building was home and workplace for the Baths Superintendent, Mr Jessop, and his family in the distant past. It comprised the house, a small indoor 'ladies' pool', and the main outdoor 'baths' and associated plant rooms. The place played a massive role in Dad's young adult years (and later, when they were courting, Mum's) and we began reminiscing about coming to water polo matches there. They played matches starring Dad and featuring a couple of uncles and lots of good friends at least weekly. Crowds were good in those pre-television days, and people loved the fierce and skilful gladiatorial contests that took place in the murky depths. They filtered the water, but somehow it was never really clear.

"Here, those two look like a couple of gorillas", a young woman commented to her female companion once when the hirsute Staniland boys (Dad and Uncle David) walked by.

"Do you mind? They are my sons," retorted my indignant Nana.

I said to the fishing boat owner, "Yes, Dad was a bit of a local sporting star in those days. George Staniland."

I could see his brain whirring as he recalled he knew of Dad,

"George Staniland", he murmured knowingly, but I was ahead of him.

"What is your surname" I threw out, knowing, by some sixth sense, what his response would be.

"Brewster," he said.

"I knew it", I exclaimed excitedly as I started told him about where we used to live on Station Street and where Mum used to come and help bathe the kids.

"Yes, yes, I remember now, a good-looking redhead. Very attractive lady."

"Yes, that was Clarice". Dad smiled at the memory.

"Mm, George Staniland," Mr Brewster repeated, "yes, Station Street."

We worked out that he would have been a young lad of fourteen or fifteen then, about the oldest of the children. Mum, just a young woman in her early twenties, probably did not bathe him!

It was an extraordinary coincidence, and we continued our chat and reminiscences for half an hour before we said our goodbyes. It was good to meet up and see how Mr Brewster and his family had risen from such early poverty.

***

Back to my early days, the 2nd of June 1953 was a date etched deeply into my memory. The day of the coronation of our new young Queen, the same age as Mum, Queen Elizabeth II. The build-up to this monumental occasion had captured the world's imagination, and it was to be the first major international event to be televised and broadcast globally. As we did not have television and would not have a set for a few more years, we trouped around to Uncle David's house on Windsor Bank to watch. There, with other friends and family, we crowded around a tiny black-and-white TV screen set in a large dark walnut cabinet to watch the historic events unfold.

I clearly remember listening to the sonorous tones of Richard Dimbleby, the renowned presenter and patriarch of what was to become an excellent broadcasting dynasty, setting the scene. The pageantry was wonderful; I enjoyed seeing the soldiers marching and hearing the military bands playing. The broadcast seemed to go on for ages, though, certainly beyond my attention span. I stuck with it though, making no fuss as I knew well by then that 'little children should be seen and not heard.'

Another occasion I remember when I should have kept quiet but did not, happened was when Grandad was preaching at Trinity Methodist Church.

Coincidentally, the tiny chapel that my grandad regularly preached at and the family attended was at the bottom of our garden on Trinity Street. Nana and Grandad were strict Primitive Methodists, an organisation like the Plymouth Brethren sect, and took their religious beliefs seriously.

I attended Sunday School from an early age, learning biblical parables and singing children's rhymes and choruses, accompanied by hand actions, led by the teachers. Also, I would occasionally come to the evening service. Grandad was very much a 'fire and brimstone' preacher and a fine orator, and in his sermons asked loud rhetorical questions as part of his delivery. I did not know that these inquiries did not require an answer.

"Do you believe Jesus will return to Boston? AND do you denounce the Devil and all his machinations? DO YOU?" he urged.

After a long, pregnant pause, I felt I had to support his cause and answered in a small voice,

"Yes, Grandad, I do."

My tiny-voiced interruption caused chuckles in the congregation and embarrassed me; I can still feel the blood rushing to my cheeks all these years later.

When we lived at Station Street, I learned to swim at around four years old. Dad took me down to the Baths, seated on a special infant seat he had fabricated on his bike. A battleaxe of a teacher taught me in the freezing outdoor water. The pool always opened in early April around my birthday when the water temperature would be, on average, a less than balmy 48 degrees Fahrenheit (9 or 10 degrees Centigrade).

Teaching, if we could call it that, comprised being towed across the pool, half the time underwater, in some sort of contraption like a leather horse collar on the end of a rope. A large, fat, shouty woman would do the pulling and instructing. Eventually, I got the hang of it, abandoned the neckband, and focused on improving my breaststroke by myself using a rubber ring initially. I found this to be much more preferable to being regularly half-drowned by this scary woman.

Another memory of my time at Station Street was occasionally going with Mum and Dad a few streets away to visit their friends Eric and Reeny. Eric was a baker, and I loved to watch him at work and smell the enticingly sweet aromas wafting from his ovens. He would, of course, spoil me by giving me slices of freshly baked cakes and sticky buns. Wonderful.

I don't remember exactly when we moved home from Station Street to Willoughby Road, but it was before I started school.

Over the other side of town, about a mile from the centre of Boston, the house was of a grey-green brick 1930s construction. It was a three-bedroom semi-detached property, on Willoughby Road fronting the Maud Foster Drain.

Maud Foster was a wealthy widow who offered generous terms for allowing the drain to be constructed on her land in return for the waterway being named after her. (Further down Willoughby Road was a windmill also named after the lady.)

Large drainage canals bisected the entire area around Boston and further afield across the Fens. The county of Lincolnshire, rather like Yorkshire to the north, was divided into three subdivisions. In Yorkshire, these were the East, North, and West Riding. In Lincolnshire, the districts were Holland, Lindsey, and Kesteven. Boston was in Holland, which took its name from the country on the other side of the North Sea. It shared many similar features with that nation: it was very low-lying, flat, and in need of constant drainage to avoid flooding.

Some 438 miles of drainage channels known to us locals simply as drains were necessary to prevent the land lying barely at sea level from becoming submerged by rivers or the sea. Dutch engineers had been involved in land reclamation schemes and the construction of drainage systems since the sixteen hundreds.

Our new house had open farmland beyond the long back garden, so I immediately had different options for areas to play. I was happy catching tiddlers in the drain, building dens or climbing the trees at the edge of the farmer's meadow.

When I started school, I walked about a mile in total; up Willoughby Road, over the footbridge across the Maud Foster, down Norfolk Street, past the Town Park, and on to the Park Board School. I returned home for lunch (or dinner, as we called it then) and back for the afternoon session before leaving for home at 4 pm. It was a tight timescale, and I was walking a good four or five miles a day as a five-year-old.

Occasionally Mum would send me to Newell's, the grocery shop just up the road by the footbridge, with a shopping list. I would hand it over to Mr Newell, who would collect each item required from various parts of his store and write the prices on a paper bag with a pencil that he kept behind his ear. When he had everything, he would add it all up.

"Two shillings, eightpence, one and nine, eleven pence. That's five shillings and fourpence altogether. Please, John," he told me. I would then hand over a ten bob note (ten shillings) and wait for my change.

I would then skip home, hoping that Mr Yates' nasty dog, a Staffordshire bull terrier, was not running loose in the dairy yard. Even when the vicious hound was on its long chain, I found passing the place intimidating. Slavering and snarling, eyes swimming with malevolent intent, it would eye me up and down, growling menacingly. This scary canine later attacked Dad as he tried to walk past on crutches, having broken his leg playing rugby. It must have been very scary even for my hero of a Dad.

Apart from having to avoid Yates' dog, I enjoyed doing errands for Mum. Sometimes I would have to take a note over to Grandma, who lived on Horncastle road on the other side of the drain. No telephones those days. It felt good to be helpful. Mum would always thank me and hug me when I got back home.

One day on my way to school I found a farthing on the pavement. This was a tiny bronze coin with a picture of a wren on the reverse side of the portrait of the queen. There were four farthings to a penny, so I went to the sweetshop where I asked for a fruit salad and proffered the money to the lady behind the counter. They sold fruit salads and blackjacks at four a penny, so my logic was that one would therefore cost a farthing. The lady let me down gently. My farthing was no longer acceptable. It was not 'legal tender' she told me. Seeing the disappointment on my face, though, she let me have one.

Sometimes after school, for whatever reason, Mum and Dad wanted me not to go home straight from school but either go to Uncle Eric's Mum's home opposite the school in Norfolk Place (the Yarnold's). Or to the Miss Simpsons' grander detached house on Friar Way, again not very far from school.

The advantage of this arrangement was that they both had television. Children's hour came on at 5 pm and, dependent on the day, offered *Rag, Tag, and Bobtail*, *Andy Pandy*, *The Woodentops*, *Bill and Ben the Flowerpot Men*, or *Muffin the Mule*. Dad picked me up in our newly acquired (but very much second-hand) Austin 7 when the programmes conveniently finished.

I found the Miss Simpsons intriguing. The two spinsters lived together in a large and most imposing detached house with a garden that went all around the property and had an extensive rear lawn backing onto school playing fields. They also had a smart black Morris Minor in the garage, registration number JL 5566, which I have always remembered.

As I worked out later, Ruth Simpson was Dad's mentor in the Post Office before retiring. He became her willing protégé as he developed the skills and experience to gain promotion within the GPO's management structure. She played a crucial role in his career development. She and Dad had a close relationship, and he helped the ladies out with jobs around the house and things like mowing the lawns. He was always grateful for Ruth's counsel and guidance.

Both ladies, Ruth and her slightly younger sister Mary, who would have been in their sixties, were very demure. Both had sprouted some wispy facial hair and had developed several tics and affectations. They also constantly went "mm, mm, mm" to themselves, but I found them both, particularly Ruth, to be kind-hearted and helpful. Mary was a bit more severe in manner, so I kept my distance and made sure that I minded my p's and q's.

I understood later that the two sisters, like so many of that generation, had lost their fiancés in the First World War, so never married or raised a family. When Dad told me, I thought about it long and hard. I felt it was an unbelievable state of affairs and so very sad.

Dawdling back from school one day, not long after the summer holidays, Mum greeted me at the front door. She was in her dressing gown and with a bundle in her arms. She was looking delighted and beaming broadly.

"Look, John, isn't God wonderful? You have a baby brother."

I thought she had been getting a much bigger tummy, and she had told me she was having a baby, but I did not know when this event was likely to happen. I did not think about it too much.

"Great, what's for tea?" was pretty much my response.

I already had a brother; I can't remember exactly when Robert turned up. When I was three, I suppose. I didn't see the need for another one, but it was probably not something I should question. I did warm to him and got involved with the cooing and holding his tiny fingers. Still, I was more interested in going out and playing football or building dens with my friends in the field behind our house than spending time with a soppy baby. He was called Richard; I was later told.

I was probably more excited another day, a year or two later, returning from school and chatting with my mate, who lived further up the road.

"Hey, John, look, there's a man on your roof!" he shouted as we neared my house.

I jerked my head upward to look up the road to see a man fixing an aerial to our chimney.

"Wow! We are going to have a telly!" I exclaimed and raced a hundred yards back home, abandoning my friend.

Getting a television was big news. We were late in having television installed, and most of my school pals already had one. My parents had never mentioned it at home previously; I think I knew better than to whinge or pester about having one - that would not get me anywhere. I felt in the words of one of Mum's favourite songs, 'Que sera, sera, whatever will be will be.' If we get one, we get one. So this installation was, to me, totally out of the blue.

The televisual experience in the fifties was miles apart from today's world of hundreds of channels, 50-inch colour screens, and HD picture quality. It was rather limited - black and white, constant flickers on a nine-inch screen, two channels, BBC and ITV, and minimal transmission times. Still, it was television and perhaps more exciting than having a baby brother.

I think it was in the Autumn of 1956 when we first got television because I have a clear memory of watching a documentary programme the next April fronted by Richard Dimbleby. He was purporting to be showing the harvesting of spaghetti from heavily laden trees in Italy. It baffled me and I remembered saying to Mum and Dad that spaghetti did not grow on trees. However, they seemed convinced that it must be true if that doyen of broadcasters said it was so. I kept my counsel, but then at school the next day, everyone talked about the brilliant April Fool joke played by the BBC. I felt vindicated.

CHAPTER TWO

FAMILY LIFE IN BOSTON

School was fine with me. I recall little about the lessons; I could readily grasp concepts in class, and the learning process did not stress me. One thing I can remember vividly, though, was a regular art lesson where the teacher would bring in a sizeable dustbin-like container with grey, cold, and delightfully squidgy and malleable clay. This wonderful material was for us to make something creative and arty.

The teacher would allow us to delve into the depths and pull out a handful of the beautiful, gooey material and mould it into something of artistic merit. The clay was not plasticine for kids but proper grownup's clay, which would go rock hard and we could then paint it. I was rubbish at making anything worthwhile, but enjoyed the feel of the stuff.

Mostly though, at school, I remember the playtimes. I liked football and playing about twenty a side with a tennis ball was the norm. You had to develop skills quickly if you wanted any time on the ball. We also played a variation of chase where, when initial catchers tagged someone, they then joined in a chain to chase down those remaining. I was invariably the last to be caught and was proud of my record! It was a pity I missed out on the dinnertime play because I was walking back from home. But it meant I looked forward even more to morning and afternoon breaks.

I always remember being almost late back to school one dinnertime and having to run down the street as I heard the bell being rung. I sprinted through the gates and got in line just in time. A teacher was at the front of all the pupils lined up neatly in form rows. She had a little girl with her who was crying and was talking gently to her. Someone had pushed her over on the playground and she had grazed her knee. The teacher asked her to walk up and down the lines and point out who the miscreant was. I was pretty dumbfounded when she stopped at me. I had been there all of thirty seconds. My protestations of innocence fell on deaf ears, and she hoisted me off for the whack with a slipper. What an awful miscarriage of justice and one that has remained with me for a very long time.

I had to stay at school one day for school dinner. I can't remember why exactly, but Mum and Dad had something special on. This turned out to be a bit of a disaster.

I did not like the food at all. It was liver and mash with onions, and the liver was hard, with bits of rubbery veins running through it; the potatoes were lumpy, and I had never been a fan of slimy onions. The pudding was tapioca, which I found pretty horrible. However, the big problem was that I had a lunchtime routine. I had developed a regular habit of going to the toilet after my meal.

So, I headed off to the outside boy's toilets and did my business. Then disaster. There was no toilet paper. I had nothing in my pockets that would do the job, so I was in a quandary. After thinking for several minutes, I realised the only answer was to use my sleeveless sweater, a favourite yellow one with red cowboys on the front. Obviously, after using it was impossible to flush, so I had to leave it all, presumably for the caretaker to sort out later. Telling my mum about the jumper episode some fifty years later, she said.

"I always wondered what happened to that lovely pullover."

Having rushed upstairs to change quickly into some old clothes to go out to play when I got home, she never realised the top was missing.

Living at Willoughby Road was convenient for playing with my cousin Keith, three years older than me. He lived on Horncastle Road on the opposite side of the drain with Auntie Muriel, Uncle Frank, his younger sister Janet (about my age), and Grandma Rowson, Mum's mum. I often walked over to play with him. It didn't seem to happen much the other way around.

If the weather was fine, we would be out playing cowboys and Indians. He would be the Lone Ranger with me as Tonto. Or he would be Kit Carson or Davey Crockett, and I would be the sidekick. He had all the gear with a cavalry uniform, including a navy blue hat with crossed brass rifles, yellow neckerchief or a coonskin cap, and faux leather tasselled waistcoat. The latter for when he was 'the King of the Wild Frontier'. I just had to improvise.

We would build dens behind a giant advertising hoarding up the road by the water tower or make daring raids on the waste bins of Fisher Clark's factory. The company made packaging and labelling, and there were always plenty of sticky labels and stacks of coloured cards which they had chucked out to purloin if we could avoid detection by the security chap.

If the weather was wet and awful, we would read copies of Dandy and Beano (he had both delivered weekly, the lucky devil) or play with our toy cars. We had Corgi, Dinky, and later Matchbox cars. His were all in their original boxes, and we played car showrooms, parades, and motor shows with them. Mine were in an old biscuit tin, and we used them for playing banger racing.

He came over to play at our house a few times in pleasant weather, I remember. He was a little envious of the vast grassy field out back, used to graze cattle. It was a great playground, with huge sycamores to climb on the periphery. Once, when we were in the field, I particularly remember some other kids coming over to mess up whatever we were doing. I used a word I had just learned and told them to

"bugger off."

Sounded good.

Keith shopped me to mum, who scolded me, and clouted me behind the ear whilst shouting about washing my mouth out with carbolic, and the next thing I knew she sent me to bed at about 6 pm on a beautiful early summer evening. The bedroom window was open, and I could smell newly mown grass and hear the rhythmic sounds of the local menfolk tending their lawns. And the laughter of all the kids, including my cousin. Funny how these things stick in your mind. Bugger.

As we now lived a fair way from Grandad's chapel, Mum and Dad found a new Methodist place of worship down Norfolk Street. I thought this was pretty cool, as there was a youth club session every week.

They cleared the main hall of seating and used the space for indoor football. We would charge around for a couple of hours, having great fun. I would then head home, grubby and sweaty, stopping off at the corner chippie for threepenn'th of chips and some free batter scraps, if lucky. This was when I was about seven years old.

I thought I should have a girlfriend at about this age and found one in the regally named Elizabeth Edinburgh who lived further down Norfolk Street. We used to walk home from school together. I decided I liked her and invited her to my eighth birthday party on the proviso that she got me a present of a pencil case with a yellow metal ruler, rubber eraser, pencils, and a pencil sharpener - the lot. She agreed and came up with the goods, which delighted me!

Daily life growing up in the fifties was quite frugal. We still had food rationing in my early years, and the Government issued coupons for essential items such as meat, butter, jam, and sugar. There were also vouchers for orange juice and cod liver oil capsules. We had to go to a clinic on London Road to get the products. This meant a long walk for Mum and me, with my brothers being pushed along in the colossal coach-built Silver Cross family pram.

Meals were utilitarian in these straitened, pre-supermarket times and the concept of eating for pleasure was yet to catch on, particularly with the lower middle classes. On Sunday, we had a small roast with slices of overcooked grey beef accompanied by mashed potato, roast potatoes, Yorkshire pudding, Bisto gravy, and smelly cabbage.

On Mondays, lunch was a few slices of beef saved from Sunday with bubble and squeak (fried leftover potato with cabbage). Mondays were also washing days. Mum would be busy getting everything in the twin tub and getting to grips with her new-fangled spin dryer before pegging everything out on the line to let the powerful easterly winds finish the job.

I call it lunch now, but we knew it as dinner then, and we ate the main meal in the middle of the day. Dad used to come home from work at 12.30 pm, and we used to eat as a family. He returned to work until around 5 pm and I was at school until 4 pm.

Tuesdays, ironing day for mum, we had Pig's Fry, a Lincolnshire speciality. This comprised various bits of pig's offal (liver, kidneys, heart, and other bits of innards fried off in flour with mashed potato, carrots, and onions).

Wednesday was baking day, and I don't recall the regular dinner menu. But I know Mum always saved me the mixing bowls to scrape out the tasty raw cake mix, complete with juicy currants and sultanas, which I loved. The sumptuous aromas of fresh baking filled the kitchen. She was an excellent cook, and we always had a stack of homemade cakes in the pantry.

Minced beef was also frequently on the menu, occasionally chops, never chicken, which was a luxury item in those days. We often had fish and chips on Friday picked up from the chippie over the footbridge or else homemade with chips coming from the battered and blackened lard-filled chip pan.

Whenever I was at home alone with mum, my brothers probably having a nap, and she was not too busy, we would dance around the kitchen to music from the radio. Paul Anka's 'Diana' Perry Como, Doris Day, and Michael Holliday went down well. She would try to get me to waltz with her to the slower music, but I never really got to grips with that.

Sometimes she would take me to Nana's on Skirbeck Road, the other end of town, just up from the swimming baths and the docks. Nana would look after me when Mum and Dad were otherwise engaged. I don't know what they were doing. I never asked, just accepting it was the way of the world. Like Mum and perhaps most homemakers, Nana was also a keen cook and very proficient at baking cakes. When she was cooking, she let me clean out the bowl as Mum did, but the bonus here was that Nana used Fussell's condensed milk in her baking. She would let me scrape the tin out and drool over the taste of the beautiful, sweet ambrosia.

I loved Nana and Grandad's little terraced house on Skirbeck Road, sadly now long since demolished. It was just two small rooms downstairs, but they only ever used the front room at Christmas. Initially, there was no kitchen and Nana would cook meals on the black cast iron range in the fireplace in the parlour. Grandad had added a lean-to extension back in the past, accommodating a basic kitchen comprising a gas cooker, sink with just a cold tap, and some rudimentary cupboards. I knew this as the scullery.

Upstairs, there were originally two bedrooms on the first floor and an attic above. Scarily steep stairs led up to the latter. The low, sloping-ceilinged room was lit with a tiny torch bulb powered by a battery pack, which failed to illuminate the shadowy, creepy corners properly. A massive feather bed sat in the centre of the room. There was no other furniture but a wooden washstand with a porcelain bowl and large jug and a vast chamber pot under the bed. The bed had originally accommodated two, three, or even more of the Staniland boys. It reminded me of the nursery rhyme where 'the little one said roll over and one fell out… etc.'

Grandad had reconfigured the floor below with a stud work partition to provide two separate rooms from the second bedroom and a narrow corridor to Nana and Grandad's room.

It was at this modest home where Dad grew up with his three brothers and two sisters. It must have been tight. There was no bathroom. There was a toilet at the end of a narrow passage at the bottom of the backyard. They hung little squares of newspaper on a nail as toilet paper.

Dad said the first job in the household in the morning when he was a boy was to carry down from the attic, the often overflowing chamber pot to be emptied into the loo.

They did basic washing and brushing of teeth at the kitchen sink or in bowls on washstands in the bedrooms. While once a week on Fridays, Grandad opened up the washhouse on the other side of the yard. He removed the substantial wooden cover to reveal a large bath. He then fired up the coal-fuelled 'copper' to produce hot water, and everyone had a bath.

On a Monday, Nana used the washhouse for its primary role, bringing into play the copper, the dolly tub, washing powder, Reckitt's blue (used for whitening clothes) and the mangle. I can clearly remember her wreathed in steam and bubbles, straggles of grey hair escaping from her bun, as she toiled to get the washing completed and out on the line in the backyard.

For the rest of the week, the washhouse became Grandad's workshop. A very practical man, he was always busying himself with some repair job or other or ingeniously fabricating something useful out of bits of scrap metal and timber.

I spent many happy hours watching him pottering around in the washhouse. He was very precise and tidy, and I remember his shelves of kidney-shaped Fynon's Salts tins neatly labelled in his beautiful handwriting with details of the various contents. Screws, nails, nuts and bolts, fixings - all properly catalogued. Tools were similarly all stored in their proper places above the workbench. He even had glass-cutting tools, which I found impressive. I didn't even know you could cut glass.

He used to whistle through his teeth as he busied himself with his various tasks, twiddling with the vice and filing something down. I used to sit on the bath cover, swinging my legs, watching and piping up with what must have been vexing questions from time to time. But Grandad would always answer patiently.

I probably should have picked up some practical skills from him, but that was not to be; it did not seem to be my natural inclination. Years later, I decided DIY stood for Don't Involve Yourself and that motto has served me well. One of my brothers turned out to be a carpenter and the other a general builder, but it would appear the practical building skills gene had passed by me.

Grandad was a wonderful, calm man, seemingly serious-minded sometimes but with a great sense of fun. Over six feet tall, handsome, sporting a white toothbrush moustache, broad and straight of posture, he used to tell me,

"Shoulders back, boy. You should be able to hold a sixpence between your shoulder blades, John."

I loved him dearly and respectfully.

When he finished whatever job he was doing, we would go inside. Nana would make him a cup of tea and give me a glass of milk. We would then retire to the parlour, where he would sit in his old and worn armchair in front of the glowing coal fire. I would sit at his feet on the little wooden stool Dad made in school woodwork classes, and we would play draughts.

I loved to play draughts with him in the early evenings, but everything came to a halt when the familiar Archer's theme tune came on the radio at just after 7 pm. This was a special time for me. He would truck with no interruptions, and I became more and more engrossed in the 'everyday story of country folk'. I have been listening on and off for over sixty years now and always think of Grandad when the signature tune plays!

Sometimes Grandad's friend, an equally impressive physical specimen who was as tall as him but even broader and somewhat stockier, Mr Kent would pay a visit. If we were playing draughts, they quickly sacrificed me, and Mr Kent took my place, not on the little stool but drawing up a dining chair. He had a booming voice, bad breath and huge hands, and he would formally greet me.

"Hello young sir, how are you this fine day?"

And we would shake hands firmly, man to man, before I had to make myself scarce.

Visits to Mum's family had a slightly different dynamic. I vaguely remember Grandad Rowson, but he died in his early sixties when I was only three, so my recollections were very sketchy. Mum said he was a very gentle man who very much loved his young second grandson, and I remember him making a fuss of me and making me laugh.

Mum's elder sister and her husband Frank, an electrician and, impressively, an ex-Royal Marine Commando in the war, had their feet under the table in Grandma Rowson's house on Horncastle Road. If they played their cards right, the modest three-bedroomed terraced house would eventually become theirs. But, I felt they had to watch their behaviour, defer to Grandma and play the long game, which proved to be a considerable number of decades.

Day-to-day life here seemed very routine, almost staid, with little fun or laughter. I recalled no other visitors coming apart from occasionally seeing Uncle Frank's sister and mother. Grandma had seriously stamped her cold, dispassionate personality on the household. She was very much the matriarch, and her word was law. Undoubtedly, Grandma had endured a tough life. She had worked 'in service' as a maid to an aristocratic family in a large country house in the Lincolnshire countryside from a young age, lost her firstborn, a son, in childbirth, and then her husband at a relatively young age. Life did not seem to be much fun to Grandma, more something to be endured steadfastly.

She used to worship regularly at St Botolph's Church, the famous Boston Stump, on Sundays. The weekly beetle drive or a game of whist at a local club on the banks of the Maud Foster drain, by the windmill, seemed to be the extent of her social life.

Grandma, to me, was a fierce and frightening lady when I was little. She showed no affection towards me. And to my mind, I felt I did not compare favourably to Keith, my cousin who lived with her all the time. One time, when I was about five, I said,

"Grandma, can you tie my shoelaces for me, please?"

She exploded. "Why can't you tie them yourself?"

"I don't know how to," I had to admit.

"Oh, come here then", she retorted impatiently and gave me a bad-tempered one-to-one lesson in shoelace tying.

I knew I needed to be a quick learner if I was not to get sharply rebuked. I concentrated and soon mastered the skill to avoid further scolding.

We sometimes went around for a meal as a family and I used to be amazed at the enormous portions Uncle Frank could consume. And the amount of salt he used to put on meals. Although he was of a slight frame and not very tall, he certainly could eat.

I used to get on pretty well with Uncle Frank, though, who had a warm and open personality despite being quite shy and did not seem to have any social connections outside of work. I think I realised early on that the women of the house ruled the roost and he seemed to keep himself to himself to ensure a quiet life. He was very good at drawing, though. I particularly remember watching him closely when I could see the small tattoo of a bluebird between his thumb and forefinger, which intrigued me, doing an excellent pencil drawing from a photograph of Boston Stump. It amazed me to see the intricate detail, the accuracy, and the way he could bring the picture to life.

Somehow, however, I felt that Mum and Dad were like outsiders at Horncastle Road, even at a young age. Visits were more a duty than a pleasure, and I felt that Dad, particularly, could not wait to be saying,

"Right, I think we must be off now," and fetching his coat.

So, we had the occasional family meals at Horncastle Road throughout the year and would visit sometime over the Christmas period. However, Mum's family did not visit Willoughby Road much, as far as I could recall. Probably not disturbing Grandma's routine would have been the reason or excuse given.

Life at Willoughby Road seemed much more fun. Mum and Dad had a busy social life with a range of friends who would pop in for a chat and a cup of tea (I was not aware of any alcohol being in the house). Many of the younger, unmarried male friends from the rugby or swimming clubs would come over often on a Sunday morning and end up playing with my Meccano construction kit or my Hornby train set.

When that happened, I couldn't get a look in. They were good fun chaps, though, and I enjoyed it when they came over. They were always around just after Christmas to see what exciting additions we had for them to play with. There was no way I could be selfish with my new toys - they were just so keen to have a go.

I also had friends to play with next door. I couldn't quite work out the relationships in the household, but there was an old lady who owned the house, and then I think Joe, a lovely chap about Dad's age who was Polish and had fought in the war, was a lodger. He had two daughters who I picked up who were Brazilian-born, but I did not know where the mother was, so it was quite an exotic and intriguing set-up. Anna was about my age and Merelka was about three years older. I went around there to play sometimes, and we always had good fun.

Several times Mum said to me whilst we were at Willoughby Road that my cousin would like me to go to the cinema with him sometimes. Cinema did not interest me and I was not overkeen as I would rather be outside playing. But I think Mum said she would like it if I went with Keith for vague family political reasons.

We saw *Reach for the Sky* when it came out, the Douglas Bader biopic, and *The Bridge on the River Kwai*, the classic war film about building the notorious Burma railway line. Keith also called for me and I went with him occasionally to the Saturday morning kids' club with a varied programme, including a cowboy feature, some cartoons, and some sing-along 'club' songs, but it was not really for me. Finding it all silly, I minimised the number of times I had to go by coming up with some excuse or other.

Mum and Dad also used to have a busy time with the formal rugby club, swimming club or GPO dinner dances, customarily held throughout the year at Boston's leading hotel, the White Hart or the town's Assembly Rooms.

On their return from a night out, when we would have had a babysitter for the evening, Mum would come in to see how my baby brothers and I were. She would wake me up, clattering and banging around in a tipsy way, I later realised, and dump a load of coloured balloons, papier mâché clown's hats, blowers, squeakers and ribbons she had rescued from the event. These I loved and treasured and looked forward to Mum bringing them home for me after a night out.

The long summer holidays at Willoughby Road were about climbing trees and making dens in the field and hedgerows behind our house with my mates from up the road. (I seemed to go over to see my cousin less and less when I became older).

We made one hideout once, accessed via an underground tunnel we laboriously excavated before covering it in old timbers and disguising it with turf on top. It was an imposing effort.

A gang of older boys from the council estate over the far side of the field once came to see what we were doing. They were looking for trouble and to intimidate us. I had a thick stave about four or five feet long. I had carved and honed the piece of wood until it was just how I liked it.

"Hey, tiddler, give me that stick," yelled one of these bigger lads.

"No. It's mine," I shouted back, "Why should I?"

"Cos I said so."

A tug of war ensued with the precious piece of wood, pulling it one way then the other, but the big lad could see that I was not letting it go. He released it. Off-balance, I stumbled over backwards, flat onto my back and my head splatting into a vast, freshly deposited cowpat. Tears and screams ensued, and a right pandemonium developed, leading to the older boys beating a hasty retreat, probably realising adults would soon come to investigate the racket. My mates helped me home, guiding me, temporarily blinded by cow shit, stinking and crying, still clutching my stick.

CHAPTER 3

HOLIDAYS, SWIMMING AND RUGBY

At weekends and in the middle of the school holidays, we would decamp to Chapel St. Leonards for a week or longer. We would stay in one of the rebuilt family-owned holiday chalets. We filled our days with splashing in and out of the sea, and charging around the golden yellow and spiky-grassed dunes. Playing massive games of beach cricket on the flat firm expanses of sand and taking the old rubber boat into the pounding waves were also great fun. All this activity involved most of our family, Nana and Grandad included (although occasionally they retired early to take a break in a deckchair). We normally gathered a motley collection of waifs and strays along the way.

After a bit of a break with soggy tomato and salad cream sandwiches on white Mother's Pride, crisps, and some fizzy pop, we - brothers and cousins and new friends as well as all the adults - threw ourselves back into the fray. We would play tip-it-and-run cricket for a while before all diving into the sea for a cool-off.

I remember Nana paddling at the seashore once, wearing a long green dress, when we were all playing around further into the sea when a colossal rogue roller crashed in and bowled her over completely. She was shrieking and laughing, but I remember the incident frightened me. Nana should not be sitting in the sea in her dress.

You couldn't stay still for long on Chapel Sands; it was usually freezing. *"Skegness is so bracing!"* was, and still is, the strapline for Lincolnshire's premier resort, which was just down the coast. In reality, that meant that vicious easterly winds, coming in from Siberia, were prone to whipping up Saharanscale sandstorms. Only occasional appearances by the sunshine to raise the mercury levels a touch required a resilient approach to having holiday fun. Despite the coolness, Dad would always insist we stripped off down to our swimming trunks, though.

"You won't get a tan with your shirt on! This is the weather that browns you!" was his mantra.

It was not until my first trip abroad as a seventeen or eighteen-year-old to the French Atlantic coast years later that I understood that the sea warmed up beautifully in the summer months in some places. I quickly realised it was possible to stroll up the beach after a dip with the strong sunshine and a balmy breeze combining to dry one's skin.

One day I remember at Chapel that they left me to my own devices for a while at the chalet when I must have been about eight. There was a small window of opportunity for me to do something naughty. I had half a crown saved up for my holiday spending. This was burning a hole in my pocket. I had spent nothing so far on the holiday because we were usually either on the beach or back at base.

Holding my money tightly in my hand, I ran down to the narrow sandy path that lay between the edge of the holiday park and the dunes. Racing past the corrugated tin shed which served as our toilet, smelling of creosote and sanilav disinfectant. I pounded the half-mile or so to the centre of Chapel St Leonards. The village centre was tiny, with a shop, an amusement arcade and an ice cream parlour, but it seemed an incredible metropolis to me.

I had once had a huge Knickerbocker Glory at the ice cream café that had taken me at least half an hour to get through. I remembered that moment as I passed the shop, but I intended to go to the previously out-of-bounds amusement arcade on this occasion. There were forbidden fruits to be tasted. I soon got rid of a few pennies in the slot machine and the crane grab machine, where I failed to latch on to anything.

Crikey, it is easy to get through your money here.

I looked for something that might be more rewarding, and my money might last a little longer. On a whim, I plopped myself down at a bingo stall where a game was about to start. The rough-looking, fat, unshaven man running the booth said,

"You want to play, son?"

and I nodded and handed over sixpence.

I did not understand the procedure and the game etiquette, but bingo is not exactly difficult. I can't remember now whether we were doing lines or the complete card, but the game transfixed me. The man kept calling the numbers I had on my card.

"House!" I shouted ecstatically.

He quickly checked my card, and indeed I had won. I was excited but also worried about how long I had been away. The chap ran through what prizes I could claim from the shelf of goodies, and immediately I saw a brilliant shiny penknife with a black handle.

"I'll have that, please, mister", I stammered, grabbing it quickly as he handed it over and mumbled

"thank you."

I was off like a scared rabbit, racing back down the path.

When Mum and Dad came back, they were not aware of anything. I had carefully hidden my penknife as I had to keep the whole thing secret.

East Anglia and the Fens area are consistently drier than the rest of the country. Although often cool, blowy, and grey, we seldom could not enjoy the beach because of the rain. However, it was raining heavily one day during our summer holidays. Dad decided we would take a quick trip up the coast to Mablethorpe and hope the weather improved later.

It did not improve. We reached the promenade area and parked. A storm of biblical proportions kicked up. Crammed into the tiny and flimsy little car, the claps of thunder and theatrical flashes of lightning were quite scary, and my little brothers began crying hysterically. Huge, mountainous, dark waves were crashing over the seawall, leaving behind sand and shells, various bits of flotsam and jetsam and huge fronds of green-brown kelp. The rain was bouncing up at least a couple of feet off the road's surface, and the wind was rocking us frighteningly. We had to stay put as it would be dangerous to drive in such a storm, so Mum broke out the ubiquitous tomato sandwiches, and we sat munching them miserably.

The weather relented within an hour, and Dad decided we would try to head back to Chapel St. Leonards. It was still raining. The car was leaking everywhere, and the wipers, relying somehow on engine revs, were not man enough to clear the windscreen, so Dad was driving half-blind. I think that was the last time I ever went to Mablethorpe.

One quite blustery day on Chapel sands, I was at the water's edge with Dad, digging some channels and building a sandcastle. Glancing up, I saw a young man at the far seaward end of one of the groynes, waving his arms frantically and shouting. However, none of the sounds were reaching us because of the wind. I said to Dad,

"Look, Daddy! That man is shouting and waving."

Within seconds he had seen what I was talking about, scanned the ocean, ripped off his shoes, threw his keys and wallet to the sand and raced into the boiling surf. I ran back up the beach to Mum, taking his belongings,

"Mummy, my Daddy, has gone into the sea with his socks and shorts on," I shouted, worried that something was considerably out of the ordinary.

My panicky face and the wallet and keys must have caused mum concern, and she grabbed my brothers, and we all raced down the beach to the water.

Fifteen or twenty minutes later, after what must have been a substantial and heroic effort, Dad struggled to the beach with two young women who were poorly. One was unconscious on one arm, and the other was over his other shoulder in a 'fireman's lift' position, vomiting seawater over Dad's back. I couldn't help but notice one of her boobs was out of her costume. The ordeal had completely drained both women's faces of any colour.

Other adults were around by now and able to take charge of the first aid process and relieve Dad of his responsibilities. After more than a few minutes, they had recovered to the extent that they were conscious, breathing unaided and sitting with towels around them. They were shivering and slowly coming to terms with the fact that they had both nearly lost their lives.

Later that evening, back at the chalet, their parents came round to thank Dad for saving their girls. I remember looking up at Dad, who was trembling with the delayed shock reaction as he spoke with them. I felt very proud that he was my dad.

Some months later, the Royal Humane Society awarded Dad a 'Certificate of Bravery'. The presentation being made by the Mayor of Boston, at some function or other. He had to go up to receive his prize on crutches, though, as he had broken his leg playing rugby a month earlier!

When we did not go to Chapel, weekends in the summer revolved around the Boston swimming club. There would be water polo matches on Saturdays and training and family swimming sessions on Sundays. I enjoyed swimming, and my strokes, self-taught, were getting better. I was also very keen to get hold of a water polo ball when playing casual games; although being so small, I had difficulty picking it up and throwing it. I persevered and improved. It was a great family atmosphere at the swimming club sessions, though with all the adults seeming to have a good laugh together. There were also enough other kids for me to play with.

My big friend at the time was David, the son of a good water polo mate of Dad's, Geoff Moulder. Geoff later became a leading local politician and served as mayor. They named the new Leisure Centre, built in the seventies, after him as a tribute for all his community efforts.

I remember one Sunday walking back from the baths just with Mum as Dad was attending a water polo meeting or something. By Skirbeck Road, a man was trying to impress a group of young women, racing along the road on his powerful motorbike. This worried Mum, as the fool was potentially putting us in danger. She made sure we were standing way to the side.

"Stupid idiot. He will come a cropper mark my words. We will stay here for a while, John."

He did a couple more high-speed passes, which I remember finding quite frightening, and then revved away beyond us around a slight corner. Seconds later, there was an almighty screech and a thunderous bang, followed by a piercing scream and loud crying and moaning. He had lost control and crashed into the front of the Magnet Arms pub, breaking his legs and badly smashing up the rest of his body.

We had to walk past the scene as the ambulance arrived. A lesson learned about the dangers of both showing off and motorbikes for me.

Soon afterwards, Bemmy Bembridge, a good friend of Dad's and a regular visitor at home, realising I liked football, said one time when he was around,

"John, it's the Cup Final next Saturday. Do you want to come over to ours and watch it?"

"Yes, please," I said eagerly, knowing he had a new (relatively) large-screen television.

On Saturday, I installed myself into a comfy armchair with a supply of cherryade and crisps (plain, of course, with the little blue bag of salt - flavoured crisps had yet to be invented) from about 11 am. This was in readiness for the 3 pm kick-off. A long day was in prospect. It was a bright sunny May day, but we had the curtains drawn to ensure no glare on the screen, a substantial 12-inch version.

I watched the coaches bringing the teams down Wembley Way and saw the players emerge down the steps wearing their special Cup Final suits. The cameras then panned around the stadium with lingering shots of the crowds and the iconic Twin Towers. The pristine, immaculately marked playing surface looked superb. There were dozens of interviews with past and current players, clips of previous finals, and a film of how the finalists, Manchester United and Aston Villa, had defeated other teams on their long journey, culminating in this day's trip to Wembley.

Of course, it was then time for the communal singing, concluding with 100,000 people bellowed out the Cup Final hymn 'Abide With Me.' The crowd then roared their approval as the two sides marched out for the presentations and the National Anthem.

It was a marathon viewing effort just to reach the kick-off time. But I found the whole occasion so exciting. Bemmy and his wife, Leila, a nurse, were popping in and out with more provisions, including lunchtime sandwiches, but they skipped the build-up transmission, which I felt somewhat sacrilegious.

A collision between rampant Villa winger Paddy McParland and Wood, in the United goal, marred the game early on. The coming together knocked the poor goalie unconscious and broke his cheekbone. With no substitutes allowed in those days, Wood had to be replaced by Blanchflower in goal. Although he returned late in the day, after being patched up, in a brave but futile effort to rescue the game.

The game seemed to whizz by quickly, with my favoured Villa coming out on top eventually through two McParland goals to a late consolation effort from United's Taylor. Wags afterwards said McParland had scored two goals and one goalkeeper to bring the Birmingham team their first trophy for some thirty years.

Eight United players under manager Matt Busby (the team, nicknamed Busby's Babes owing to their relative youth) lost their lives the following February in the Munich air disaster. However, remarkably, the club reached the 1958 final as well.

My interest in football, particularly in the romance of the FA Cup, had been well and truly pricked. In December of that year, a friend invited me to go up to Darlington to watch Boston United play the north eastern town side in one of the early rounds of the following year's competition. I did not know where Darlington was, but it seemed like a good idea, and I remember pleading with Dad to let me go and being pretty upset when he wouldn't. My friend reported it was a good game, although Boston lost 5-3.

I watched the 1958 final again at Bemmy's. This time, the opposition was Bolton Wanderers, with the England Star Nat Lofthouse leading their line and scoring twice, netting the game's only goals. The second was controversial with the muscular Lofthouse bundling the United keeper, the Munich hero Harry Gregg, over the line with the ball. In those days, goalkeepers were not the protected species they subsequently became, so the goal stood.

May and the FA Cup Final month, was also when they held Boston's vast, sprawling and famous May Fair. It was so big that it took over the whole town centre, Wide Bargate, Narrow Bargate, the Market Place, the Five Lamps area, and beyond. Lasting the entire week it was brilliant fun. They formed it from several travelling fairs coming together. It was a hugely prestigious and popular event, a true highlight of the year for Boston and the townspeople.

It was so exciting, and we boys had saved our pennies to get ice creams, candy floss, and best of all, mushy peas with salt and vinegar. We couldn't wait to enjoy it all.

The fair had everything. A helter-skelter, dodgems, waltzers, an enormous Ferris wheel, a cakewalk (my favourite), sky boats and loads of stalls for hoopla, rifle shooting, test your strength, tin pan allies, hot dogs, candy floss and toffee apples. There was even a boxing booth where young men who fancied their chances could take on the resident pugilist.

There were baby rides for my brothers as well. I loved the noise and smells from the massive throbbing diesel engines, tasting the warm fumes, and hearing Buddy Holly and Elvis blasting out on the PA systems. It was just so brilliant.

We would all trek up as a family and stay well beyond dark, tiredly walking home down by the Maud Foster, still finishing our mushy peas and clinging on to our coconuts and goldfish.

***

We seemed to get extreme winter weather in Boston. The easterly winds coming over from the Russian Urals brought plentiful snow and ice. The drains would freeze, and a broad expanse of water around Cow Bridge, a couple of miles from home, would become a vast ice rink and hockey pitch. Mum and Dad's gang of friends would throw themselves enthusiastically into fun speed skating events and casual ice hockey games at the weekends. I would mess about at the edges, sliding around in my wellies while looking after my brothers (to a degree).

I conducted a small experiment one day when supposedly looking after my baby brother, who was in the pram. How far would I be able to tip the pram until he fell out? I reached an impressive angle until I found substantial additional proof of the theory of gravity. He didn't need to make such a racket, though.

The snow seemed to hang around forever, and we used to play in the field out back, have snowball fights, and build snowmen. The teenager who lived up the road built a very impressive igloo one time, which lasted for months.

With my winter sports programme, what frustrated me was the lack of any hills for sledging. Grandad had made me a brilliant wooden sledge with stainless steel runners, but there was nowhere to take it for a decent, speedy ride. I caught my Dad at a moment of weakness, and I must have pestered him a bit, and he agreed to pull me behind the car. Health and safety had yet to be invented, so this seemed a perfectly acceptable outcome. I remember one cold, sunny and snowy day having a brilliant time being towed up and down the road. It only happened a few times more, though, and I think Dad reflected on whether this was an appropriate course of action. Or, more likely, Mum had put her foot down and put a stop to the fun on 'health and safety' grounds.

I had to walk to school and back through the snow and ice four times a day, which I found was perfectly ok. However, a lady who lived close to the footbridge, and obviously saw me trudging along the road, took pity on me and kindly presented me with a balaclava she had knitted for me. "This should keep you nice and warm, John," she declared as she presented me with the woollen head covering one day to keep me protected from the cold.

On cold, long winter evenings, I was happy to go to bed early and get comfortable under the covers. I could lose myself in a fictional world of the Famous Five or the Secret Seven, Enid Blyton's children's classics. Often continuing reading with a torch even after Mum had shouted up,

"Lights out, John."

As well as May Fair and summer holidays, Christmases, when we were at Willoughby Road, always stuck in my memory. They always seemed to fit a regular pattern. On Christmas Day evening, after a day at home with our new toys and a family lunch, we went to Nana and grandad's celebrating with all the aunts, uncles, and cousins, a mix of boys and girls. The evening at Nana's meant being in the front room for the only time in the year playing silly games organised by Dad and Uncle David. Two of these I remember were Nelson's Eye and Submarines.

The first involved younger family members being blindfolded and being brought into the room from the hallway where they were waiting to be called in. Dad would then take the victim's hand, saying;

"We are doing a bit of a history lesson here" and asked them if they had heard of Admiral Nelson; of course, they said

"Yes" and allowed themselves to be moved gently to where 'Admiral Nelson', or Uncle David in disguise, was sitting.

"Well, we have Lord Nelson here now; you can touch him carefully."

He was on a dining chair, wearing a jacket with some brooches and badges pinned to his chest to represent medals. He had left one of his arms out of the jacket sleeve. Guiding their hand, Dad allowed the person to confirm a person was there, touching his head and chest. Dad would adjust his spiel as necessary depending on the age of the victim and picking up from answers they gave to the question.

"What do you know about Admiral Nelson?"

"Well, he was a fearless naval commander, and he lost his arm in battle."

"Yes, very good! He was indeed an authentic hero, very courageous, and he won lots of medals for valour. He is wearing them now. You can feel them," he said, taking the hand and allowing the young cousin or whoever to feel the baubles on Uncle David's chest.

"And, as you rightly said, he lost an arm," he continued, "this is his good arm," leading the hand to feel an arm that was in the jacket, drawing out the drama.

"And this is his bad arm,", guiding the hand to the empty sleeve to confirm there was indeed no arm inside.

"Do you remember anything else?"

"Yes, I think he lost an eye."

"Very good. You know your history, clever girl!"

"You need to be careful here," Dad said, easing the hand towards Uncle David's face and feeling an eye cautiously.

"This is his good eye. Be very gentle."

Then, quickly taking the forefinger, continued,

"and this is his bad eye," thrusting the finger into an especially squidgy orange with a finger-sized hole in the middle.

Cue screams and squeals and laughter all around.

The other prankish game, submarines, involved the prey being told they were doing a rapid-fire observational game. Lying on the floor on their back, they had a coat placed over them with the sleeve over their face, so when someone held it up they looked upwards as if peering through a periscope. Dad would then pass several household objects quickly past the sightline and ask them to say what they saw. He would show a cup, fork, a tin of soup and pretend the scorer was marking down the results of their efforts. The climax was showing a soup ladle, and when they had answered,

"Ladle,"

he would quickly flip it over to send a stream of cold water down the periscope.

"And what's that?" Cue lots more hilarity.

Games over, there was a massive spread of food as a buffet laid out on the living room table. Nana had set out the baked ham, cheeses, cold turkey, bread rolls, and salads alongside nuts, oranges, tangerines, dates, and a trifle. There might have been the odd glass of sherry, but that would have been the extent of any alcohol.

Boxing Day daytime was at home with the three of us boys playing with our new toys or building Meccano models in the front room. Sometimes some of Mum and Dad's friends would pop in, and the men would commandeer the Meccano and Hornby again. I was getting used to it by now.

In the evening, we walked over to Uncle Walter's house in Wormgate, part of the old medieval centre of Boston very close to the Stump. Uncle Walter, the oldest brother, had initially been a plumber but then got into the painting and decorating business. Eventually, he bought a large shop to sell wallpaper, paint, and some household and fancy goods. Above the shop was a spacious flat, which was a great party venue. This Boxing Day gathering was essentially an adult's party, though. They banished cousins to a large back room with loads of pop and crisps and left to our own devices.

Cousin Barry, three years younger than me, Uncle Walter's son, used to have cases of soft drinks delivered weekly. George Brocklesby, 'the pop man' who had his own business and was coincidentally a stalwart of the swimming club, ensured there was a plentiful supply.

On another of the days around the Christmas period, there would be a large gathering at Aunt Edie and Uncle Art's. Uncle Arthur, always known as Art, was Nana's youngest brother. He was a market gardener and had a small holding out at Wyberton, in the middle of the Fens and just up the road from my birthplace, Wyberton West Hospital.

He had a few acres of arable land, some pigs and chickens, and several large greenhouses for salad crops and houseplants. Their house was modern and large, with a huge farmhouse kitchen, two other downstairs reception rooms, and even a downstairs toilet (or 'cloakroom' to be posh). They had plonked the house in the corner of his land on a narrow road flanked by drainage ditches. The road twisted back towards Boston, where you could see the Stump rising majestically out of the murky, flat, landscape. His son Peter, who worked with uncle Art and was a decade younger than dad, had his bungalow, recently constructed, on the other end of the field.

Aunt Edie was a larger-than-life character, roundish and jolly, almost Dickensian, with red cheeks and a raucous laugh. Mum and she got on very well as they both had a great sense of humour. With Aunt Edie in charge, parties were brilliant fun with bountiful homemade food and manic games like charades and murder in the dark.

When I was around nine, I went to help Uncle Art from time to time in the holidays and he paid me the princely sum of a florin (two bob or ten pence in 'new money') for a day's hard labour. The worst job was being out on the ice-encrusted, rich, chocolate-coloured but bitingly windswept land, picking sprouts for the day. I had some fingerless gloves to ward off frostbite, but I could never get warm.

As I occasionally stood up straight to stretch out my aching back, I would look up to the big skies; grey, cold and threatening, extending over the flat, treeless, arable, and somewhat melancholy landscape, before resuming my bent-over duties. I reflected I was working hard for my money, but concluded that hard work was no bad thing. I seemed to have a strong work ethic at an early age.

When my travails were over for the day, I would try to thaw out in front of the roaring Aga in the kitchen while eating one or two of aunt Edie's homemade scones with strawberry jam. Ecstasy.

A much better job was dibbing out geranium cuttings in the warmth of one of the greenhouses. Uncle Art showed me how to take offcuts at the right point, dip them into the purple potassium permanganate and plant them in new pots. It was a little tedious. But it was warm and quite cosy, and I could allow my mind to wander and daydream about more fun times ahead and how I would spend my vast wages.

We spent winter Saturdays when the icy conditions allowed down at the Rugby Club. As far as I recall, the club offered very little in terms of facilities other than about three windswept pitches, a training area, and a basic changing hut, but no showers. I watched Dad for a bit, but then grabbed a spare ball and played a game of touch with a few young mates whose fathers were also playing.

The small crowd, limited to a few hardy souls, was the 'two men and a dog' scenario. It would often include Basil and Dick Clark, the club's stalwarts, committeemen, and wealthy owners of Fisher-Clarks, whose factory I used to raid with my cousin for sticky labels. Ernie Bridges, a successful potato farmer who would often bring Dad a sack of spuds, was also a regular. He had a blue Ford Pilot car which I thought of as pretty posh. I had travelled in the vehicle occasionally, but the soft suspension always made me feel queasy, and I had to concentrate on avoiding puking up.

I remember after games going back to the White Hart hotel in the middle of Boston, which had suitable facilities for sports teams. These included a large communal bath out at the back of the place.

Occasionally I would go with Dad. It fascinated me to go into the changing rooms with the raucous jovial noise, discarded kit, boots and bandages on the muddy floor, the strong acrid smell of liniment. Steam would spiral up from the massive white-tiled square bath, and the boisterous laughter and singing (particularly after a good win). With just a towel around their waists and swigging from bottles of beer, the motley choir would reel off an extensive repertoire of songs. They would belt out, one after the other, tune after tune, in a well-practised medley, many of which should not have been for my ears.

I would sometimes get to the Club bar at the White Hart with all the men before Mum came to pick me up and take me home.

They would buy me crisps and lemonade whilst they tucked into foaming pints of draught beer.

At the end of the season proper, probably in May, Boston RFC played in several seven-a-side tournaments around the county. I remember these being good fun with a coach trip, singing and laughter, and lots of rugby action. The best tournament for me was at Skegness, where we could combine a seaside trip with the rugby event. I think Mum used to take my brothers for a stroll down the long promenade, maybe go on to the pier or play on the beach with buckets and spades. But I would typically opt to stay with Dad and the rugby men.

At the end of the competition, there would be a presentation to the winners in the colossal canvas marquee, beer flowing, and more singing. One particular occasion I can remember was when the men completely festooned my jerkin in multi-coloured beer bottle tops. The men had fastened them using the cork from the backs to secure them and provided me with an impressive and colourful suit of armour.

Skegness also featured at the other end of summer. Early September always saw the Lincolnshire swimming and water polo finals held at the enormous outdoor lido on the seafront. One of the largest in the country, the swimming pool was a hundred and ten yards long, with two shallow ends and a deep central area with diving boards. It was here that they positioned the floating, full-sized deepwater polo pitch.

The occasion drew enormous crowds of East Midlands holidaymakers from Leicester, Derby, and Nottingham, filling the tiered white concrete seating. The visitors enjoyed watching swimming races and some serious high diving from the 10m platform.

Comedy antics, in routines produced by many of the polo players and the divers, followed the more serious sport. Many of the men dressed in old-fashioned Victorian swimming costumes and wigs and put together a spectacular and raucous display from the top board. I remember Uncle David being an outstanding diver and a leading light in the comedy stuff as well.

The water polo final inevitably featuring Boston with Dad as captain was the highlight of the gala. They also invariably won.

I watched and avidly cheered as Dad steered them to victory, leading by example with a few goals.

Being held in the early evening in September meant that the unheated pool was more than decidedly chilly, and I remember freeing myself from Mum's grip to see Dad. The Mayor of Skegness had just presented him with a vast trophy, not unlike the FA Cup, and having handed the prize to teammates, was sipping a cup of tomato soup to warm him up. He was very much in danger of spilling it all over himself; he was shivering so much. I looked up at him, and he smiled and hugged me, and I could feel his body trembling from the cold.

CHAPTER 4

MOVING TO CHEADLE

Often on a Sunday afternoon, the family would go for a walk, and my favourite one would be to follow the tidal River Haven and take a loop to walk around Boston docks. As a boy, Dad would always explore the port area, and I think he used to enjoy it as well. I found it quite exciting reading the ship's name, looking at the flags on display and working out which country they were from. Checking whether there were any banana boats in the harbour was something I always did as well. The Geest Line vessels were regular and frequent visitors. Shouting up to sailors on deck, I would ask if they had any foreign stamps that I could have. Ships from Holland, Germany, Belgium, Scandinavia, the Baltic countries, and Russia docked regularly, and I would always get a supply of postage stamps to add to my collection.

We also used to walk at Fishtoft, down the Haven bank, and around Freiston Shore, which I found to be powerfully atmospheric. With the vast grey skies dominating the low landscape, the screeching of the seabirds on the salt-laden wind, and the enormous ploughed expanses of rich brown arable land beyond, they seemed to be bleak, and melancholy places but with a certain touch of ethereal beauty.

I think Dad felt very close to Boston and the surrounding landscape. It was very much a part of his soul, but he also seemed a little restless, thinking there was a big wide world beyond the Lincolnshire fens.

When I was nine, Dad came home one day and said he was in line for a promotion at work, which would mean moving away from Boston. I think I had realised by now Dad was ambitious in a quiet, determined way. However, this was a move abroad to a place I had never heard of – a British Protectorate called Aden.

Dad said it was a hot, dry place, effectively a desert land, but it sounded exciting to me. It would mean going on an aeroplane, something I never thought I would do.

I dreamt that night about flying for many hours and landing in a hot sandy place where we queued up with our cases to go through a turnstile and on into a dusty town of low, white buildings (like in my illustrated bible). There would be loads of camels and thousands of Arabs milling about. Dad had been in the Middle East in the war and had brought back a complete outfit of flowing white djellaba and a black coiled thing called an agal that kept a cloth covering over the head. So I knew a little about how Arabs looked. Whenever there were fancy dress functions, and there always seemed to be several throughout the year, he would go as a Middle Eastern gentleman. He would wear this regalia set off with a dark pencilled-in moustache.

Unfortunately, Dad did not get the job. I say, unfortunately, but in reality, his failure to land the position saved the family from spending a few years in what was a pretty desperate place. They commonly knew it as the arsehole of the world.

But I found the prospect of moving away from Boston to be exciting. I embraced the concept of living somewhere else, making new friends, and enjoying many more varied experiences. It would happen soon enough.

Dad was actively seeking to move up in the world, though, and before long told us they had appointed him Postmaster of the GPO in Cheadle Staffordshire. I had never heard of the place, but it was a small market town a dozen miles east of Stoke-on-Trent and bordering on to the Peak District National Park. His appointment was quite an event, as he was to become the youngest postmaster in the country.

They sent me off in the Easter holidays for a couple of weeks to stay with Auntie Hilda and Uncle Don and my three girl cousins. Anne was a similar age to me and her sisters, around the same as my brothers. I think Dad must have driven there, but I don't remember clearly. I was just excited about going. They lived in suburban Stanmore, Middlesex. Basically, this was the big capital city. London. How brilliant!

I was being packed off out of harm's way while Mum and Dad dealt with all the logistics involved with the move to Cheadle and looking after my little brothers.

Stanmore was close to Heathrow, and it fascinated me to see the great airliners taking off and landing in a regular sequence. Zooming off to places like America and Australia. Maybe I would get to fly one day. I hoped so.

The Griffiths lived in a modern suburban semi on a cul-de-sac opposite a park. There was a school at the end of the road. About half a mile away, was a 1930s row of shops and a tube station. An actual London tube station.

The girls were fine, and I got on with them ok, but they were girls. I was keen to play football, and I used to go over to the park and hang around where older kids played until they relented and let me play. My birthday was when I was staying in Stanmore, so I had just turned 10.

Wearing some new grey jeans, which I thought were cool, I quickly realised I should have been in shorts. I ended up with grass stains all over them. The older boys accepted me over time, although initially, they banished me to being the goalkeeper. I later persuaded them to let me play outfield and was proud to overhear one lad say,

"This kid can play a bit, Mike!"

I went to the park most days after that.

It was a bit of an eye-opener to live for a couple of weeks in a different household. Auntie Hilda was perhaps ahead of her time regarding her attitude to healthy eating and would give us muesli (which I had never heard of) for breakfast. We also had brown bread with honey, fresh fruit and orange juice, which I had not had before.

For some obscure reason, I also remember chatting with my aunt about the function of the human appendix.

"Oh, it does nothing; it's just from when we were apes." She stated glibly.

Knowing that Nana and Grandad were very much in the creationist camp, I felt this Darwinian viewpoint was quite controversial.

I enjoyed chatting with Auntie Hilda, who was unafraid of expressing her opinions and happy to discuss a range of issues.

This was something I did not come across in our home life, where there was not that much conversation about current affairs or other matters of interest.

After my period of London living, it was time to return to the family and our new house in Cheadle. Mum and Dad came down to drive me back up north, leaving my brothers with our new neighbours.

It was all quite exhilarating as I would also go to my new school, Cheadle County Primary, at the end of the three-week Easter holidays.

My first impressions of our new home were very favourable. It was quite a large, handsome, detached, pebble-dashed property with a garden that went all around the property. There was a garage and an imposing copper beech tree at the front – hence Beech Cottage's name. It reminded me very much of the Miss Simpsons' place in Friar Close, back in Boston.

The place inside, though, was a bit of a mess. There were cardboard boxes, packing cases, and tea chests still awaiting unpacking. The house looked like it needed decorating throughout. I decided some of the paintwork would have to go because it was a horrible, dowdy, dark green colour. The complete house would need a thorough cleaning, and initially, I was reluctant even to touch the disgustingly greasy door handles. There was also a disturbing, musty smell about the place.

Mum and Dad had done a lot of work already and had decorated the bedrooms, but there was still much to be done.

We boys, though, thought Beech Cottage, had a significant and very attractive feature. The original front room was to be given to us as a permanent playroom. The family living room, a sizeable room with French doors out to the garden, was a relatively new feature built as a side extension to the house. There was also a separate dining room, a large kitchen, a downstairs loo, an upstairs bathroom (how posh!), and three bedrooms. It was great – or would be soon.

The garden was brilliant, not huge, but with plenty of room for ball games plus, there was an orchard belonging to the next-door neighbours directly behind. This was potentially suitable for scrumping, exploring, and making dens in.

The house was very well located, just up the hill from the High Street so that mum would send me down to the Co-op for bits of shopping.

"Make sure they put the 'divi' on John, and they write it down on Mrs Staniland's account."

The shop was one of these new self-service places where you walked around putting groceries in a wire basket. You then handed it all to the lady to ring through the till. It was a bit more modern than Mr Newell's shop in Boston.

Mum and Dad seemed thrilled with the house and that they were forging a new future away from Boston's sometimes oppressive and parochial atmosphere. It did not take long for them to get it shipshape. Dad had to cope initially with getting to grips with his new job and then coming home to spend evenings rubbing down and preparing surfaces, painting or hanging wallpaper. Mum was also being heavily involved with decorating. They made a good team. Mum, to me, seemed to be particularly happy with this new life in Cheadle with her husband and her boys.

I remember being asked to help with the wallpapering one time by Dad when Mum was out at a new friend's, and I found it so excruciatingly dull. Dad was good but slow and very particular, so most of the time, I just seemed to stand there waiting. Or else holding up a piece of pasted paper at arm's length until I thought my limbs would drop off. After that, if Dad asked for help, I would make myself scarce or volunteer my middle brother, who was far more practical than I was. That seemed to be the answer.

It was soon the end of the Easter holidays. At least I had had a few days to explore my new surroundings, but it was almost time for Robert and me to start our new school. He would go to the Infants section and me to the Juniors. It was a straightforward route of around a mile down Tape Street. We walked separately with our new friends early in our school careers.

This new phase of my life was positive and exciting for me. I only had the summer term before the long six-week holidays, and then, when I returned to start the new school year in September, I would be a Top Junior and prepare for the 11-plus examination.

The first few days were a little weird as I became familiar with the new surroundings and systems, the quirks of the new teachers, and, of course, getting to know my fellow pupils. This meant quickly assessing who could be a buddy in the future and who I should best avoid.

Initially, they gave me the moniker 'Yank.' I had explained on being questioned by a group of kids where I had come from; the only Boston they had heard of was in the USA. Ignorant peasants. It also helped them come up with a nickname for me because I had recently had a crewcut hairstyle that was very American. The Yank thing only lasted a few weeks until I became Stan, obviously from my surname, which I found much more acceptable.

As I believe one would expect with ten-year-old boys, there was occasional banter bordering on bullying from time to time, but I could hold my own. Occasionally there was the odd bit of shoving and pushing and shouts of "Fight! Fight!" ringing out through the playground, some of which I was central to, but nothing much came of it. We played mass football games with a tennis ball at break times, and I think other players recognised my ability at the game and this helped me become accepted.

I remember early on being set upon by two or three bullies from the top class who, after roughing me up in the cloakroom, buttoned my blazer up and hoisted me onto a peg, leaving me dangling and helpless. They left me suspended by my collar with my feet waving a foot off the floor. Nobody was around, and I shouted for 'help', which brought the Deputy Head from the Staff Room to rescue me. I didn't snitch, though.

Dad was keen to join the local Methodist Church, which we did early in Cheadle, and we attended Sunday School regularly and the evening service. I made good friends with two older lads, Keith and Alan, who were second years at Uttoxeter Grammar School. There was also a family of two girls and a boy, Jen, Ken, and Lesley, who were a little older, and another family around the same age, the Staniers. The chapel became a big part of our social life.

After a few weeks of walking down together as a family for the evening service, I persuaded my parents to allow me to walk there with my friends and sit separately in the upstairs balcony area. They gave me sixpence for the collection, but I bought two ounces of pear drops on the way and just put a three-penny bit in the offertory. Fair enough, I thought. The pear drops would just about last the service out.

Our little gang knew we needed to be quiet and at least give the appearance of listening attentively to the sermon. However, we were intent on discreetly passing brief notes between ourselves and trying not to titter.

Once Mum and Dad had finished redecorating the house, it looked extremely spick and span. I was proud to live in such a stylish home. Dad now wanted to get back to playing water polo again. He found a club at Hanley, one of the five towns with Burslem, Tunstall, Longton, and Fenton, which made up Stoke-on-Trent. I used to go ten miles with him to training sessions on Tuesday evenings, watch matches, and practice my swimming and water polo skills. We also joined the Stoke-on-Trent Post Office Sports and Social Club, which staged several social events over the year and had regular family swimming sessions on Friday evenings at Burslem baths. The whole family would enjoy swimming or throwing a ball around, taking part in fun races and socialising with friends. We would finish the evening off with fish and chips on the way home, which would be a highlight of the week.

Saturdays quickly became my favourite day of the week as I would walk down to the Recreation Ground, the Rec, and meet up with friends to play football all day. We would divide into two teams and play on the whole pitch, even if we were only half a dozen on a side. We would often play 'ten half-time, twenty the winner', so changing ends when one side had scored ten goals and then playing on until a team had reached twenty. Taking a break, we would go to the shop at the side of the park for a 'lubbly jubbly'. This was a frozen orange juice in a pyramid-shaped carton with virtually no calorific value at all, but which would somehow sustain me all day. No wonder I was a skinny kid. After the brief interlude, we would mix the teams up a bit and start again.

In the summer holidays, football still reigned supreme, with only a short period in August when we gave cricket a bit of a chance.

Saturday teatime, I would wearily dawdle back home after football, the mile or so up Tape St, but seemingly further on the return journey. I would be sweaty, muddy, and quite exhausted. Once home, I would wash my hands and face, and possibly wipe my knees, before gobbling down my tea. I would then launch into an orgy of television-watching with the rest of the family. We would see the *Six-Five Special* with Pete Murray, Don Lang, Wee Willy Harris, and the crew, followed by *Dixon of Dock Green* and then a Saturday night family special like *The Black and White Minstrels Show* or the *Perry Como Show*. Mum used to love the latter, seemingly quite taken with the smooth-crooning American.

In our first summer at Cheadle, Mum and Dad were keen to explore the beautiful countryside around us. Many people have a preconception of Staffordshire as being a heavily industrialised area with endless rows of grimy soot-stained back-to-back houses and a landscape of lots of factory chimneys belching out toxic fumes. Stoke itself, with its worldwide reputation for high-quality porcelain and pottery, particularly evoked images of industrial decay, shabbiness, and deprivation. There were parts of the county where this viewpoint might have had a ring of truth, but we were only a few miles from the beautiful rolling hills of the Peak District. East of Cheadle, attractive little villages and exquisite rural idylls like Dove Dale, Ilam, the River Churnet, the Manifold Valley and especially pretty spots like Dimmingsdale dotted the countryside.

It was all so different from the flat, treeless, arable landscape around Boston. I knew that Mum, in particular, thought this chance to appreciate 'proper countryside' with trees and hills was terrific. I believe she enjoyed Cheadle more than anywhere she ever lived.

The first summer we were in Cheadle, and in subsequent years, we had Nana and Grandad, the Miss Simpsons' and Grandma visiting at various times. We would take them out to enjoy the rural panoramas, take short leisurely walks, in deference to their age and mobility, and have a picnic tea of sandwiches, cakes, and drinks Mum had prepared. I think when Grandma came to stay, it would be an enjoyable break for Uncle Frank and Aunt Muriel back in Boston.

All our visitors appreciated the beautiful area in which we now lived. We would head off to explore the area in the old shooting brake vehicle that Dad had picked up. I thought it was a little shabby and would have liked us to have a smart new saloon. But, to be fair, it was a highly practical vehicle for family weekends.

The five of us, (when we did not have visitors), plus all the picnic paraphernalia and bats and balls, could all pile in with room to spare. We would find a suitable spot in a field, close to woods and rocks for exploring and climbing, and set up camp. First, Dad would despatch me to find some suitable flat stones to build a hearth. Once I had completed this task, I would be off to collect some kindling and larger logs for the fire. He would then light the sticks to get the fire going and sort out the cooking arrangements. Tipping out the range of soot-blackened and battered pots and pans from the white (well, originally white) canvas ex-navy holdall. Then he would busily prepare our campfire meal. Not the most creative cook, Dad would focus on producing sausages, eggs, and beans. Mum would butter bread rolls and set out homemade cakes.

We three boys would then run off and play, build dens and climb trees and rocks until being called back to eat.

We would then demolish plates of food with cake and bread and jam for afters. After our meal, we would be off again, leaving Mum and Dad to relax and have a bit of a break from dealing with three demanding young boys. Not that relaxing, though, sometimes.

I recall one time we were all climbing up some quite impressive craggy outcrops when my middle brother suddenly shouted out,

"I'm falling!"

He had time to yelled, but inexplicably not the time to put his hands out to break his fall. He went six feet straight down and rather unwisely broke his fall with his nose. Dad came running over in response to the yells and crying. Once he had calmed him down, he assessed the damage, got hold of the seriously misplaced proboscis, and clicked it back into an approximately central position. Later, the doctor told Dad he could not have done better himself, and his prompt attention had left my brother with a commendably straight nose.

49

CHAPTER 5

A DIFFERENT SORT OF LIFE

For our holidays now, we could look westwards rather than east. We were in the middle of the country, around eighty miles from the sea, but it seemed the world was now our oyster. It was not just the bleak, windswept Lincolnshire coast that was on offer.

Wales was now our number-one pick for holidays. In late May, we went away in what we then called Whit week for a few days and then had a two-week break in the middle of the school summer holidays. I remember staying in a catered farm cottage at Saundersfoot near Tenby, a caravan at Llanaber near Barmouth, and another close to Porthmadog on the Lleyn peninsula. After that, camping was the holiday of choice. Perhaps cost came into the decision-making process; maybe accommodating a growing family of five in a caravan was too much, or there was more freedom with camping.

I know Mum and Dad did not like that at Saundersfoot, we sometimes had to leave the beach early on a glorious summer's evening. This was to avoid being late for the meal that the farmer's wife would have prepared. Camping gave us much more flexibility, and if the weather was great, we could stay on the beach as long as we wanted.

We first pitched up in Mr Jones' field in the middle of Anglesey, the large island off North Wales' coast one Whit week. Very basic camping was the order of the day, with no facilities other than an outside toilet and a standpipe in the farmyard. Dad had acquired a large, full-height ex-army ridge tent while I had my own tent, bought as a present, that I would erect alongside. The family was very much about beach holidays rather than touring around and sightseeing. When camping, we would trek off to the beach daily after breakfast. On Anglesey, as we were camping right in the centre of the island, at Mona Farm, Dad would look at the sky, feel the breeze and listen to the weather forecast on the radio before deciding which from a choice of half a dozen beaches would suit us best that day. The tiny hamlet where we camped was actually on the trunk road, the A5, which bisected the island and ended a few miles onwards, to the west at the port of Holyhead.

The family's favourite beaches, without a doubt, were Newborough and Llandwyn Island. Accessed down a mile-long gated forestry commission track, once off the narrow twisting lanes, I would run the final leg opening and closing gates to allow Dad to drive down the rutted sandy trail continuously. I enjoyed running and saw this as part of my training programme to become physically fitter and stronger.

Once parked, we were all loaded up with picnic stuff, towels, a large sack of beach games, and sun loungers. Dad would heave a large bag that held a heavy-duty inflatable rubber canoe he had bought second-hand onto his shoulder, and off we would go. We would walk the entire length of Newborough beach, an incredibly empty vast stretch of sand, listening to the waves crashing in and breathing in the salty ozone. We would walk along anticipating a full, fun-packed day of play. Occasionally, when taking a short rest break, we would look over our shoulders at the magnificent spectacle of the mountains of the Snowden range away to our east, on the mainland over the Menai Straits.

We were aiming for the small white lighthouse we could see half a mile or so in the distance, at the point of a small peninsula that was Llandwyn Island.

I think Dad had spoken with friends and colleagues from the Head Post Office in Stoke about Anglesey, and some of its wonderful beaches. He also pored over maps in the evenings, while sipping his coffee, planning routes and potential destinations.

We regarded Llandwyn as our special place, and we barely saw anyone else on our regular excursions. One day my youngest brother, running ahead as he was unencumbered by any carrying duties, breathlessly reported back,

"Daddy, there is someone on our beach!"

How dare they?

We would set up camp on a little sandy beach at the edge of the little peninsula, a spot brilliantly located for exploration of the rocky outcrops and the many sheltered inlets. At the end of the so-called island, more of an isthmus were the pretty whitewashed lighthouse and a couple of little keepers' cottages.

Exploring, climbing, rock pool investigation, beach cricket, swimming, going out through the waves in the canoe, and eating our picnic would keep us busy all day until the sun dipped into the sea.

Our beachside activities would always involve Mum and Dad, maybe they would just take a quick break on the loungers after lunch, taking time out for 'forty winks'.

Even if it were a little cool and overcast, Dad would still insist on us stripping off to our swimming trunks all day, claiming,

"This is the weather that browns you." Just as he had done years previously at Skeggy and Chapel St Leonards.

That would be his stock phrase, as he was quite a sun worshipper.

I, with my freckly complexion and auburn tinges to my dark brown hair, used to get burnt in the sun if not careful and required the regular application of Dad's patent sunscreen and tanning lotion. Essentially, this was a mix of olive oil and vinegar. His homemade solution saved a few bob towards the holiday budget. There would be no way he would squander hard-earned cash on some fancy Ambre Solaire.

A few years later, when I was in my teenage years, I sometimes found it challenging to make an impression on the girls I met on the beach when wandering around smelling like a bag of chips.

Back at base, after a long day, we would play around our hilly gorse-covered camping field and climb the rocky outcrops until Mum called us in for tea. She had collected tins of stewing steak and tinned vegetables over the past few months to make camp cooking more straightforward. We would also have plenty of homemade cakes to enjoy as dessert.

There was a chip shop in Newborough village, and probably once a holiday, or maybe twice if lucky, we would get a fish supper on the way home as an exciting change.

***

When the nights were drawing in at the end of summer and into autumn, we used to head out to Oakamoor, just a few miles out of Cheadle on Sunday mornings. Above the village was a densely wooded area with an ample supply of dead wood.

We would pile into the ancient grey shooting brake, Dad, Frank, the henpecked husband from next door, and we three boys to go logging. We had two open fires at home and we would try to build up a good supply to keep us going until spring. I would have to help the two men, being older, whilst the other two just played at making dens and charging around.

Collecting sacks of decent kindling was my primary duty. Dad had developed the incredible skill of spotting substantial dead branches amongst the fully mature trees, lassoing them with a weighted line, and pulling them down to chop and saw into logs. Frank was not a lot of help, seeming just to hang around until the Rising Sun opened at 12 before nipping off for a quick pint.

Dad and I would load the back of the vehicle to bursting, and then around half-past twelve, we would all pile in and head back home after picking Frank up from the pub.

I remember one time when I climbed a tree at Oakamoor I became stuck at quite a height. It was on this occasion that I realised I could not always rely on Dad to get me out of a tight spot. I found the situation scary and shouted for help, thinking that Dad would be able to somehow magic me safely down to the ground. After a while, I knew it was a problem I would have to work out for myself; he could only encourage me. I learned an important life lesson that day. Self-reliance.

On our return with a load of timber, I would love to open the back door to savour the delicious aromas of Sunday roast. Mum would be in the kitchen, with pots and pans noisily bubbling away on the stove, mixing the gravy and popping the Yorkshires in the oven, music playing on the radio and would yell,

"It's nearly ready now; just wash your hands and sit down at the table."

Or

"It'll be ten minutes; you've got time to stack the wood."

And we would all respond accordingly.

Billy Cotton's Band Show, raucously introduced by the eponymous bandleader himself with a rousing "Wakey, wakey" or Family Favourites would be on the radio, the BBC Light Programme. We would then all sit around the dining table to enjoy the culinary highlight of the week.

A roast joint of meat with Yorkshire puddings and all the trimmings and piles of vegetables would disappear in no time.

Mum would then serve sponge pudding and custard or apple and blackberry pie up for afters, and this would disappear as quickly as the main course.

"All morning to prepare and gone in seconds", Mum complained jokingly as she surveyed all the empty plates.

The funny thing I remember, though, about family meals was that we did not talk. I always felt that it seemed logical that it would be an excellent opportunity to chat about many aspects of our day-to-day life when we were all together around the dining table. Every time I tried to start a conversation, though, I was told,

"No talking at the table."

I don't know why this should have been, perhaps, something from their childhood, particularly in Dad's strictly religious family regime. I never understood this rule but had to accept it, but it made me a little frustrated. It was very different at Auntie Hilda's.

The radio and Billy Cotton's blathering seemed acceptable, but not normal family conversation. I did not understand.

Dad did not hold strong views on current affairs, it seemed to me, and would not express opinions about anything contentious. He was very much about consensus and was not happy dealing with anything controversial. I would have been comfortable talking about issues in the news or different aspects of the political world, but it was not to be. I sometimes flicked through his News Chronicle and wanted to raise some social or political issue, but he would shoot me down quickly.

The policy certainly changed when I had my family years later, and Mum and Dad happily embraced the convivial and chatty tables we presided over. However, again, they would avoid controversial subjects.

After lunch, we all had to have our regular baths (if we needed one or not). We would then put our best togs on and head off for Sunday school.

Our neighbours on the one side were Frank and Poppy, their little girl and an elderly grandmother. We did not have that much to do with the family and would just see Frank on our Sunday morning logging excursions. I don't know how that came about, but I am sure it was just an excuse for him to have a crafty couple of Sunday lunchtime pints.

Our neighbours on the other side were Brian and Margaret and their new baby Jane. Both our houses had side doors that faced each other's kitchens, so communication was much more frequent and straightforward here. On the other side of their house was the commercial part of their property, Stoddard's Garage, which did the usual vehicle repairs and servicing and was also a fuel station.

On the other side of the building, there was also a wide track that extended quite a way down to a more expansive parking area that housed their fleet of ten tonners used for sand and gravel haulage. This was the mainstay of their business. Brian was a Stoddard. His father, Percy, or old man Stoddard, as we referenced him, had established what was now a thriving business before the war.

A widower, he lived over the other side of the road with the younger bachelor son Malcolm. The vast, prominent house at the top of the hill dropping into Cheadle town centre was a grand old white stucco home with extensive grounds hidden by high, dark wooden gates. Old Percy, ruddy-faced and white-haired, in his sixties, appeared to be a cantankerous, highly successful business owner, and very prosperous. He also seemed to be someone not to cross. I was messing about on an old broken-down truck on his land at one time when he caught me. He certainly let me know what for, as he forcefully remonstrated with me in his basso-profundo voice, his face spittle-flecked as he verbalised his displeasure, steam coming from his ears. I was very careful not to annoy him again.

Brian, his brother Malcolm and other drivers the company employed did regular stints, taking loads of sand and gravel from local quarries to Stockport and other places in south Manchester.

Brian was a quiet and friendly chap and offered me the chance to be the driver's mate on a couple of trips, which I took him up on. But sitting in an uncomfortably bumpy and funereally slow wagon on a prolonged trip up north was not my idea of a fun day out. When I politely declined to go on any more sorties, my brothers were both keen and became regular passengers on the gravel lorries during the school holidays.

Margaret had grown up a dozen miles to the east out at a village called Waterhouses on the main Leek to Ashbourne road, in the middle of the beautiful Peak District countryside. Her dad had a dairy farm. Because of her agricultural background and love of all things to do with the farming way of life, Margaret had dragged Brian along to Cheadle Young Farmers' meetings. She later encouraged me to go along to talks, quizzes, and social evenings. It was not my thing, but it was very kind of them to think of inviting me along, presumably for me to broaden my social horizons.

I remember going to one regional Young Farmers event with them. There were several agriculturally slanted competitions and events; They totted up marks awarded to decide on the overall winning team. They were short of someone to go into the Herb Identification event, which was quite self-explanatory, so Margaret browbeat me to fill in.

"But I know nothing about herbs," I protested.

"You'll be fine. I will just walk past and whisper to you."

Inevitably, it was a disaster. I wandered around cluelessly, examining the various green and often pungent exhibits and scribbling something down on my notepad with Margaret sidling up to me and whispering thyme or basil or whatever. She was spotted and unceremoniously evicted from the room by a stern middle-aged lady judge. This mortified me and had to continue to complete my assessments with a very pink face. I think I failed to trouble the scorer when I handed in my sheet somewhat sheepishly.

Occasionally, they would need me to babysit for Jane when they went out for an evening. I was very young to be entrusted with such responsibility, being only ten, but I suppose they thought I would be ok. If the baby awoke, I could readily nip back home to alert my mum if required.

Later that first summer, Margaret arranged for me to spend a week helping her father on the family farm. I stayed in a vast bedroom with a huge feather bed and sheepskin rugs on the bare floorboards. We took meals at the old oak table in the homely old farmhouse kitchen with a large cream Aga keeping the place cosy.

I was up with the cockerel helping Margaret's amiable, ruddy-cheeked, grey-haired and bewhiskered dad with the cattle, the ducks, sheep, and chickens. It was good fun if hard work, and after a long day outside and a classic home-cooked meal and a brief sit down in front of the fire, all I wanted was my bed.

One day I found a few hen eggs in an obscure spot where they had obviously been for ages. On a whim, I flung one at a barn wall where it exploded with a pleasing bang and gave off a pretty impressive authentic stink bomb aroma. So, I carried on with the rest of them. Good fun.

Back at school that autumn of 1959, I was a top junior, and schoolwork seemed very focused on the 11-plus examination at the end of the year, determining whether I went to Grammar school. I was very keen to get to Thomas Alleyne's Grammar School in Uttoxeter, where my friends Keith and Alan were already in the third form. There were other options. Longton High School in Stoke and Leek Grammar were also choices, but I had set my mind on joining the boys.

I can clearly remember our form teacher that year, although her name has slipped my memory. Attractive, elegant, and dark-haired, she seemed quite sophisticated, like a film star. When the bell went for break or lunchtime, she would always reach for her handbag and take out a distinctive red flatpack of extra-long Du Maurier cigarettes in readiness for a relaxing smoke in the staffroom.

She was firm and very much in control as a teacher, but friendly and approachable as well. My friends and I worked out quickly that she had organised the classroom so that the brighter kids were on the right of the room facing the front, the not-so-clever ones on the left. We did a lot of mental arithmetic, and our first row was always the one shooting hands skywards, keen to be asked for the answer. We quickly realised that she did not always invite us to respond; the teacher knew we were ok and intended to draw some answers from the other side of the classroom.

We also did a lot of chanting out in a rote form of learning (it was the old pounds shillings and pence back then) twelve pennies one shilling, twenty pence one and eight, thirty pence half a crown, through to eighty pence six and eight and ultimately to two hundred and forty pence one pound. When we did this, the most confident voices came from our side of the classroom. The teacher would listen out on the other side of the room to pick out the quiet ones.

She later introduced us to some test books in arithmetic, intelligence, and English comprehension, which were in the same format as the 11-plus examination. We would work our way through those. The teacher spent time with the children struggling with some concepts, but our side was pretty much left to our own devices, devouring the test papers with relative ease.

One day early into the new term, at playtime, there was a group giggling excitedly around a boy who had a copy of a tabloid newspaper, the Daily Mirror, I think. He was reading out a salacious story relating to the death of film star Errol Flynn. The article was of growing interest to boys of our age group as it focussed on his alleged sexual prowess and the impressive size of what the journalist coyly referred to as 'his member'. When the story related accounts of Flynn's swordsmanship, they were not referring to the flashing steel blades he employed in his portrayal of Robin Hood.

A week earlier, there was a group of boys again discussing the news. I was completely unaware, but there had been a General Election where Macmillan's Conservatives had won a landslide victory and gained an increased majority of a hundred seats in the Commons. I knew nothing of politics and so when one lad said, "Who do you support, Stan? Conservatives or Labour?" I just replied Conservatives, as it sounded better. I remember feeling very under-informed.

One enjoyable event, one not involving blatant cheating, I went on with the Young Farmers was a day trip up to Blackpool by a coach that autumn. Blackpool was a holiday mecca for people in the North. We would take in the funfair, see a show, and then take the slow late-night procession down the seafront to see the famous illuminations before taking the long drive home.

We spent a couple of hours at the fair, trying out the various roller coasters and other rides. Later, we would try our luck on some sideshows before having fish and chips, along with countless other high-spirited visitors, as we walked along the seafront.

I remember finally going on the very new Wild Mouse ride, a very scary wooden roller coaster with Margaret. I felt very queasy and was not overly keen to repeat the experience.

The live show a little later was probably the first time I had been to a theatre, and I enjoyed it immensely. The headline was comedian Al Read with Irene Handl and many glamorous dancers, singers, and speciality acts.

It had been a full day, but I was looking forward to the illuminations. Unfortunately, I fell asleep on the coach before we started down the promenade, and neither Margaret nor Brian saw fit to wake me. I awoke halfway back home in the middle of the night, wondering what had happened to the highlight of my Blackpool visit. I was not best pleased.

***

Back at school, we spent most of our time in class with our form teacher, but we got a change of scene when we had music with the Deputy Head. As he was a leading light in the town's Gilbert and Sullivan Society, music lessons became an appreciation of the light operetta genre. This did not bother me, as I liked the tunes and the clever lyrics. I even persuaded Mum and Dad to take me to see whatever the Society was performing at the Town Hall that season.

These particularly witty words, from the Mikado, I have memorised now for over sixty years: '*To sit in solemn silence in a dull, dark, dock, awaiting the sensation of a short, sharp, shock from a cheap and chippy chopper on a big, black block.*'

Out of the classroom, I loved playing football at break time (when not reading racy news articles). One day the headteacher surprised me by coming across as we were playing and asking to have a chat with me. Wondering what on earth I had done wrong, I walked over with him to the covered walkway that looked out over the playground.

"John, I think it is about time we formed a football team to play against other schools. What do you think?"

"Yes, sir! That would be great."

"Very well then. I want you to be my captain, so let's have a look at who should be on the team."

So, for the rest of the break time, the master and I selected the likely contenders.

"Jonny Myatt's a good little player, Michael is big and strong at centre half, Pete's very nippy with a good shot, and Piggy's a great goalie."

"Piggy?" the Head queried.

"Sorry, Colin, sir", I clarified, giving the proper name for a boy with a harelip who everyone knew as Piggy.

We picked a team and organised a couple of practice sessions at the Rec over the road. We thought we were not too bad.

Over the next couple of months, we were going to play a few games. We were all looking forward to the contests and taking part in a proper match with a referee, a leather ball and goalposts with nets.

We did not exactly set the world on fire, losing both games by the odd goal, but I remember thinking it was great to be playing proper competitive football. It was something I could look forward to more of if I got to Uttoxeter.

One of my school teammates, Jonny Myatt, a talented footballer, seemed to seek my friendship around this time. He was a shy little lad and normally lived on the other side of the classroom. He did not find schoolwork that easy.

One day at break, he came up to me after a maths lesson and confessed,

"I didn't understand a word of that stuff on fractions, did you, Stan?"

"Yeah, it was ok. What don't you understand?"

"All of it," he muttered disconsolately.

"I tell you what, Jonny, I'll pop around after school and see if I can help," I replied.

I knew he lived only a few hundred yards from me, out on the road out to Alton.

We walked home from school later and down to his house, a tiny two up two down terrace. Jonny's dad was a coal miner.

There were still a few working pits in the area. He was not bringing in a great deal of money, judging from the home's appearance.

The door opened onto a front room directly from the street. It was devoid of any furniture except for an ancient pram sitting on the bare floorboards in the corner. That was all.

Jonny called me through to the living room where his mum was sitting on a stool in front of the black cast iron range on which a kettle was boiling over the glowing coals. She was cooing and shushing a fretful baby. A filthy little toddler wearing just a nappy was crawling around on the bare floorboards.

He introduced me to his mum, who greeted me with a weak smile and a quiet,

"Hello, John."

Jonny signalled to the dining table and chairs, the only other furniture in the room, and we sat down.

It did not take me long to explain the fractions he was having trouble with, and I could soon leave and head off home.

"Bye Mrs Myatt, bye Jonny, see you tomorrow," I threw over my shoulder on leaving.

I walked home thoughtfully, thanking my stars that I was not living in such a way. The abject poverty the family was enduring shocked me to the core.

I told Mum about it when I got home, and she listened patiently and said she would sort out some clothes we had all grown out of which might be suitable for the baby, toddler, and even Jonny.

***

I was still doing plenty of swimming, picking up some water polo skills, and watching Dad play in the league for Hanley most weeks. Dad had quickly slotted in well, as a key member of the team and scoring plenty of goals. The family swim sessions on Friday nights were also great fun, and we all made some good friends.

Mum and Dad did quite a lot of socialising with friends from the Post Office and chapel, going to dinner dances and quizzes and such, leaving us in the charge of a babysitter for the evening. They deemed me capable of looking after baby Jane next door but not organising my brothers. Probably a fair assessment. The babysitting nights led to us all, including a young babysitter watching the telly throughout the evening. Until we heard the car pull into the driveway when we all skedaddled to bed.

I also started going to the weekly youth club that had started up at our chapel, where we chatted, played table tennis, and listened to the latest pop records on an old gramophone. Some people brought their records to play to hear the latest sounds from Cliff Richards and the Shadows, Buddy Holly, Tommy Steele, Paul Anka and Del Shannon.

Walking home after Youth Club, some of the gang had smoked. It did not appeal to me, but there was undoubtedly some peer group pressure to give it a go, so I tried one. I wouldn't say I liked it at all; it made me cough and splutter and tasted disgusting.

Once home, I was so sure that I stank of smoke that I raced upstairs and brushed my teeth vigorously before casually going into the lounge to greet Mum and Dad. I got away with it!

We had settled well into life as a nuclear family in our new home. I could feel that my parents were happy that they had made the break from Boston and that their focus was now on their three boys and giving them a secure, loving upbringing.

Mum had joined the Townswomen's Guild and had a good friend there called Kath. I am sure that she was revelling in a bit of independence and a chance to socialise with her group of friends.

I always got on pretty well with my brothers, but I found I had little in common with them because of the age differences. They played together with their toys in the front room while I lay on my bed reading. I was three years older than Robert and five and a half in front of Richard. If I were around them, I would tease them constantly. Though, I would usually be out playing with my mates if I wasn't reading.

We were all very respectful to our parents and would not dream of being anything else growing up. Occasionally we were naughty, but it was all sorted out with a stern word and a threat of a smacked bottom if we persisted. I remember one evening, when we boys were all in bed, with Mum and Dad just relaxing in the lounge, I pushed things a bit too far in provoking my siblings and they started making a real racket. They shared the large front bedroom, while I had my own smaller room at the back. I would go into their room and chuck something at them or flash the lights on and off.

"John, I know what's happening. If you carry on, you will feel the weight of my hand on your bare backside."

I could not resist having another foray into their room with the same result. The next thing I knew, I heard Dad charging up the stairs two at a time and yanking my bedroom door open. With one continuous movement, he pulled back the covers, turned me over, pulled my pyjama bottoms down, and, with a hand the size of a dinner plate, laid into me half a dozen times. The resounding smacks stung, but I held back the tears.

I think I learned the boundaries after that minor episode.

The first Cheadle Christmas came around, which was a hectic time for Dad as he had to organise extra temporary staff for the incredibly busy Christmas period. As the boss he was in charge of a substantial operation, ensuring that the local townspeople and businesses received all their presents, parcels, regular mail and Christmas cards promptly and that people could pick up their stamps, pensions, and postal orders at the busy counters. He also had many rural sub-post offices under his control that he had to visit and check regularly.

He had also roped in Mum to do a few sorting shifts as a paid employee (some independence and Christmas money for her, which she enjoyed). She would also regularly make large batches of mince pies for the postal delivery workers over the period, which was to become a tradition and always went down very well.

In those days, the community considered the position of postmaster as having some considerable standing in the town. Dad's firm, fair and very capable approach and Mum's willingness to 'muck in', for example, doing the sorting shifts, having a renowned sense of fun and, of course, producing constant batches of mince pies, helped in breaking down any potential barriers of 'us and them'. I could see they were both viewed with a lot of respect when I occasionally visited his workplace.

I think Dad must have quietly been quite proud of what he had achieved. A good job, a delightful house, and lots of good friends. The scholarship boy from Boston Grammar, the third son in a family of six of an illegitimate jobbing lorry driver/yardman and a poor fisherman's daughter from Norfolk, was now the youngest postmaster in the country.'The boy had done good.' Life was going nicely in Cheadle.

CHAPTER 6

A CHEADLE CHRISTMAS AND UTTOXETER GRAMMAR

Dad was working long hours throughout December, and inevitably, visiting Boston for the holidays would not be possible. It was a significant break with tradition, not travelling to Lincolnshire to join in the extended family celebrations. But I felt we were all ready for this turn of events. We were a family who would enjoy our Christmas together with our local friends.

The chapel had a lot going on over the festive period, with the Sunday School putting on a Carol Service and seasonal bible readings. I was singing a solo, 'Once in Royal David's City' and doing several recitals. So there were practice sessions for those, and with school events and parties, a lot was going on.

Mum, particularly, seemed proud of my inaugural stage performance as I sang the carol in front of a packed house.

That Christmas, my best present, was a proper leather football. My parents could not readily disguise it, even when wrapped, and it was at the top of my pillowcase. They crammed the latter with gifts, chocolate selection boxes, nuts, and tangerines that I could feel with my feet at dawn on the 25th. Squeals of delight came from my brothers' room, so I knew they were awake as well. Opening all my other presents was great, but just loved the rich, earthy, sweet smell of my leather football and could not resist regular sniffs throughout the day. I was longing to get down to the Rec to give it a tryout.

It would just be our little family group this Christmas Day. We boys were in the playroom; Mum was preparing lunch, and Dad helping Mum a bit while ensuring that we had a lovely blazing log fire we could gather around later to play games and watch some festive television. It was all quite perfect, and I even stopped teasing my brothers for a while.

I think we visited Boston for subsequent Christmases once Dad was confident he could take a couple of days off. We stayed at Nana and Grandad's and enjoyed the festivities as we had in the past, but that first Cheadle Christmas etched a place in my memory. I can recall the warm, cosy, festive atmosphere and the overwhelming emotion of being loved and enjoying being in the family's bosom.

We had a few days before we were back at school after the main festivities of Christmas and the chapel's special events were over. These were spent down at the Rec with my new ball, referred to as a 'casey' (as in leather-cased ball) by all and sundry. It was so much better than the light Frido balls we usually played with, although it could get heavy when wet. Making sure I always dried it out properly, pumped it up, and applied dubbin, I tried to keep it in top nick.

The plastic balls we had previously used would puncture easily, which sometimes meant games had to be curtailed while we undertook emergency remedial work. The repair involved a delicate process of heating a spoon on the gas hob and applying it to the plastic to melt a small area and spread it over the puncture. It took a certain amount of skill and did not always work, but it could prolong the life of the ball. Having my casey meant this was not an issue anymore.

Back at school, it was all about doing endless practice for the 11-plus. It was getting tedious, but eventually, the day when we would sit for the examination came around. Having prepared so thoroughly for this event, I was quietly confident of passing and looking forward to joining up with Keith and Alan at Uttoxeter in the next school year.

Over Easter, a year after we had first come to Cheadle, we had Nana and Grandad come to stay. I remember Dad taking them out to Dimmingsdale at the perfect time to take in the unrivalled display of colourful rhododendrons that were a seasonal feature. They loved their brief holiday with us and the chance to see more of our wonderful and varied countryside. So different from Lincolnshire.

School after Easter was a bit of a non-event after the examination that had dominated everyone's thoughts and efforts for so long. But it was still a great relief to get the news that I had passed and I was on my way to Thomas Alleyne's. I was also told I would be in Class 1A, the top stream.

They allocated me to Kitchener House, which was yellow or amber, and although I would have liked to be in Flint (green) or Phillips (red) like Alan or Keith, it was not a big deal. The colours were necessary for certain aspects of the school uniform, including the scarf, which Grandma Rowson, a fearsomely industrious knitter, started on immediately, and thoughtfully, to have ready for my first day.

I missed watching that year's FA Cup final in May for some reason or other, Wolverhampton Wanderers won, which pleased a couple of my schoolmates who were Wolves fans. However, by chance, a month later, I just turned the television on at the right time to see what was, and still is, unquestionably one of the best games of football ever. Hampden Park, in Glasgow, hosted the European Cup Final. The giant ground held over 127,000, an unbelievable figure, to watch Real Madrid in their 5th successive victory beat Frankfurt Eintracht 7–3. There were mesmeric performances by several players, including the wizard of a winger Gento. None performed better though than Puskas, dubbed the Galloping Major by the press, as he was in the Hungarian army and the Argentinian Alfredo di Stefano. They scored all their team's goals, with Di Stefano netting four times and Puskas three. At the end of the game, I just thought, *Wow. I am pleased I saw that!*

I can't remember where all the other kids from my class were going the following September, but only four of us went to Thomas Alleyne's, and only one, Michael, was going to be in my class. Some girls were going to Uttoxeter High School, next door to the Grammar School. Other pupils who passed the exam were presumably going to Leek Grammar or Newcastle under Lyme, which were the alternative choices. If they had failed the test, they were off to the local secondary modern next to our current school.

That summer, being more aware of what went on in the area than the previous year when we were just learning the ropes, we attended many local village fetes.

Our own Cheadle fete was a great example. These local celebrations were not like anything I had experienced before; they were large-scale productions, starting with a vast carnival procession through the streets led by a brass band at the front of the parade. Female marching display teams with various themes and uniforms, street entertainers, stilt walkers, fancy dress competitors and elaborate floats sponsored by multiple local businesses and organisations followed on. The pageant would end up at the recreation ground where, with pop music blasting out of huge speakers, there would be vast numbers of stalls and sideshows, fairground rides and attractions, hot dogs, and toffee apple stands. The organisers had staked out a sizeable area of the park pitches as the performance arena for bands, display teams, dog shows and agility tests.

When the various constituent parts of the parade had arrived at the rec, the Mayor, with the beautiful young Carnival Queen alongside him, formally opened proceedings. Mum and Dad, my brothers and I then walked around, taking in all the sights and sounds and absorbing the distinctive aromas of candy floss, grilled burgers and diesel fumes.

However, the big attraction of the fete for me was the children's running races, for which there were cash prizes. They were to be held a little later, and I couldn't wait. I was a speedy runner, and the idea of being able to win the princely sum of half a crown for success in a sprinting event had me drooling.

The time came for the races, and I was champing at the bit as a sizeable crowd gathered at the edge of the straight track marked out in clean white lines, contrasting with the green turf. Nervous, but quietly confident, I shot off at the gun to win all three races I was eligible for by a margin. Think of the money! Fortunes!

After my first taste of success at our home event in Cheadle, I was hooked. The Mayor handed over little brown envelopes of cash after the races, and I couldn't be happier.

Races over, we continued to explore the various stalls and watch the displays of the marching girls. This I found immensely captivating, particularly the team dressed as cowgirls in short yellow skirts and fringed leather waistcoats singing Doris Day's 'Deadwood Stage.'

We bumped into the beautiful young carnival queen, a girl of around fifteen, in all her finery, standing with her mum as we walked. Dad spoke to the older lady as he knew her. She worked at the post office as a cleaner. As we stopped for quite a chat, my friends Keith and Alan passed by and said hello. Their eyes were popping out as I introduced them to Jill, the lovely young lady, and they looked across at me with a nod of respect for making the introduction.

Over the next few weeks, I insisted we trekked out to the local villages of Kingsley, Froghall and Dilhorne to attend their fetes. I added to my cash balance with running victories plus picking up a couple of lesser place cash prizes for the fancy dress competitions dressed up as a clown or an Arab. I wasn't keen on the fancy dress routine, but it was still a nice little earner.

Our major summer holiday again that year was a two-week trip to Anglesey. The journey seemed to take forever, travelling the length of the A5 northwest to Mona.

As always, we had a full and enjoyable holiday on the beach, or if the weather was not so good, looking around the little market town of Llangefni, which was close by. Or perhaps visiting South Stack lighthouse or clambering around the lovely Beaumaris Castle overlooking the Menai Straits.

What always amazed me when we returned tanned and refreshed from the holidays was that Dad, just a day before, looking bronzed and fit and charging around, playing beach cricket in his swimming trunks, suddenly transformed into the professional man he was. On Monday morning after the holidays, he was in his suit, freshly ironed white shirt and stylish tie, ready for action.

For us boys, it was still some time before we had to go back to school. As they were now a little older, my brothers used to attach themselves to me more. I was still playing a lot of football (and a little cricket) at the rec when I didn't want them along. But I was happy for them at other times to join the gang.

Our little group, mainly from the chapel fraternity, but including locals from the council estate, where Keith, Alan and the Whitefields lived, were happy building dens, exploring and running around as kids do. Beyond their homes, it was all countryside. When we went through a gate, we were into farmland, where a pretty little brook meandered across the field. The stream's width went from a modest couple of yards across to a more challenging three or four.

Brook jumping was a popular game where we all followed the leader who chose where and when to jump, and we all followed. As the age range went from fourteen-year-olds to five-year-olds (my little brother), this was fraught with difficulties. I tackled all the jumps the big lads took, but there were a few mishaps and soakings amongst some others, particularly the youngster.

We also used to walk up country lanes about two or three miles to High Shutt and the National Trust area, Hawksmoor, opposite. Playing pretend battles and building dens in the bracken was brilliant. This was even though signs had been erected warning of adders being in the area.

At the top of High Shutt was a large foreboding, and lone pine tree, on a raised piece of common land, visible even from Cheadle. Locals said the tree possessed a strange power, with generations believing that if one walked around it nine times, it would occasion the sound of bells summoning death. I wouldn't say I liked to dwell on that fact. Others said that in the past it had been used as the site for hanging captured highwaymen.

Towards the end of the holidays, when the blackberries were out, the posse went out to play but had to pick the fruit first. I had a small ex-RAF rucksack that would hold two large cylindrical tins that once held a baby's milk powder. Mum required me to have these filled with blackberries before we could do our usual stuff. It was worth it, though, as it would lead to lots of blackberries and apple jam and pie fillings to last us over the winter.

On rainy days we used to go round to someone's place (not ours as we did not have a record player) and stack up a dozen singles onto the record player and listen to them constantly. I liked Buddy Holly songs and lots of the American pop tunes of the time. Del Shannon's 'Runaway' was a great tune.

The summer holidays were soon over, and it was time for me to start at Uttoxeter. I had my PE kit and smart blazer labelled up with Cash's name tags. The company called 'Cash' produced rolls of embroidered name tags, which mothers had to spend hours sewing on to uniforms and PE kits. I also had my new scarf courtesy of grandma, some new black and white 'continental' football boots, a little tin box with a protractor, set square and compasses and some new crayons. Mum had bought me a lovely burnished leather satchel to put stuff into.

On the first morning, just before 8 am, wearing my new junior school tie in the Kitchener colours and school cap sat on my head, scarf around my neck and satchel on my back, I headed off just a few yards down the hill to the bus stop. A few different school buses plied the route to Uttoxeter. A couple went via Tean on a more direct route, or there was the circuitous country route through Alton, Oakamoor, and Rocester. They had allocated me to the longer rural bus journey.

The direct road was about ten miles; our route probably doubled that, but I didn't mind as I knew most of the way well; it was beautiful countryside, and it made for an interesting journey. We picked up clumps of other pupils of various ages and sizes at several villages before reaching Rocester.

At Rocester, we passed the JCB factory, where they made the shiny yellow earthmovers and diggers. Older boys introduced the new kids to the daily sport of identifying as many of the rep's cars as we could see in the car park to the front of the building. Bamfords had cornered the market in the JCB registrations, and over the coming months, we ticked off JCB1 through to JCB13.

Shortly after, crossing the A50 bypass, we headed into the pleasant little market town of Uttoxeter.

Several fine old buildings that made up the venerable institution impressed me when we finally reached Alleyne's Grammar School. We walked through the ancient and substantial wooden gates into the quadrangle. Immediately to the right was a sort of chapel building, which was the modestly sized school hall. In front of that, behind an imposing brick wall and solid full-height double wooden gates, was the head teacher's house.

School prefects from the upper school organised all the newbies and showed us around the teaching buildings in small groups before depositing us in our classroom. Our particular guide explained that the school day would usually start with a Head's assembly in the school assembly hall, but not today.

Opposite the Headmaster's house on the other side of the quadrangle was an old two-storey building with a classroom for technical drawing on the ground floor. A large woodwork studio took up the upper floor. Further along were the changing rooms and toilets.

At the far end of the quad was the main school block, a two-storey edifice of somewhat newer vintage than the rest of the buildings, but still probably over a hundred years old. This housed a range of classrooms, laboratories, the Head's Office and the Staff Room.

To the side of this building was a long narrow passageway that led to a large playground with two low-level prefabricated structures to the right. 1A was to be based in one of these rooms.

On the far side of the broad tarmac playground was another low, modern building: the school dining hall and kitchens. An enormous playing field lay beyond the dining hall, along with a wooden pavilion, and an open-ended brick building I learned was the fives court. This was not a game I had ever heard of, but would quickly understand.

It was not a vast school; there were only about 350 boys, but it felt right. I was sure early on that I was going to enjoy my time here. It was all so new at the moment and the prospect of discovering what grammar school life was all about over the next few days and weeks excited me.

I might have attended the school in its 400th year; I only missed the anniversary by a couple of years. Thomas Alleyne, a wealthy man of the church, left a sizeable legacy in 1558 to provide for a new grammar school. The original school had been elsewhere in town, but had moved to this more sizeable campus in the mid-1850s.

For the first hour, we were with our form teacher in the prefab classroom where we would go each morning for registration and conduct various administrative matters, like the collection of dinner money, we were told. The teacher wore a formal academic gown and mortarboard, which quite took me aback. I had previously seen only such attire on Jimmy Edwards' *Whack-O!* television show.

The teacher organised us alphabetically; He had put our names on little typed cards on each desk.

We then had to answer the register and on this first occasion had to give our full names. The boy behind me had the second name of St. John, of which I had never heard. I think the teacher was a bit confused as well, as the poor lad had to state and restate his name a few times,

"S t dot, J dot", he kept stressing.

"Idiot", he muttered under his breath.

Then the form master handed out 'rough books' for all our notes, homework details and instructions. We were told to use the pencil on the desk to write our names on the front of them. We were also told to note how to spell the word 'Grammar' on the front cover. It was a heinous crime to get this spelling wrong by putting an 'e' instead of an 'a' at the end of the word.

In the first form, we were to use pencils. Staff would only trust us to use pens when we reached the second year. They would then provide basic nibbed pens, which were to be dipped into inkwells I had noticed built into the right-hand corner of each desk.

We then had to write out our timetable with the details of the day, time, subject, teacher and classroom. It was to be something new - constantly moving around the school between different classrooms.

After more administrative detail, the master announced a break, after which we were to go to the designated classroom according to our timetable.

We raced off; me hoping that a bit of a kick-around on the playground might be possible.

My satchel was on my back with the long straps going under my arms and up around my neck.

I had not seen Keith or Alan earlier as they travelled in on the other bus, but they spotted me at break and called me over. They were 4th formers now and wore the proper grown-up ties, not our funny little junior ones.

"John, why have you got your bag on like that? You look a right prat. Give it here," said Keith.

Confused, I handed it over, and with that, Alan had whipped out a penknife and cut the strap down so that it was very short. He thought he could improve my shiny new satchel with some more knife slashing and further enhance its appearance by the application of some ink from a bottle that had suddenly materialised. They then kicked the offending article around the playground to give it a good scuffing. Some of their mates joined in to 'help'. When the school bag had been, in their estimation, sufficiently distressed, they gave it back to me.

"There you go, that's better."

This mortified me. Mum would kill me. But I could see what they were trying to do. Cruel to be kind, you might say. There was no malice, and it was not bullying, although their efforts had not thrilled me. Wearing the bag like I was, signalled 'new boy'. They were trying to get me fast-tracked into acceptability by the older lads. My satchel now looked like the scruffy items they carried.

We spent the rest of the day going to different classrooms and meeting various subject teachers who handed out textbooks and exercise books that required marking up with our names. It would be confusing for a while to get to know the drill, but I knew it would soon become routine. Some masters wore the gown and mortarboard, whilst others went for the sports jacket, leather patched elbows, and slacks look. (There were no female teachers on the staff).

One of the formally attired teachers was the headteacher, Mr White or Chalky, behind his back. Thomas White, his son, was in our class.

Mr White was to teach Latin in an old-fashioned high-ceilinged room with metal and wooden desks with a built-in bench seat arranged in rows on tiered wooden platforms. He rapidly distributed texts and exercise books, almost flinging them at us.

"We should not waste time. We should get on with learning some Latin from the outset."

He started by explaining the meaning of our school motto, Nisi Dominus Frustra, *Without God all is in vain,* and then rapidly turned to the blackboard and scribbled up Amo, amas, amat, amamas, amatis, amant. "First conjugation amo. I love." And then, pointing at the words with a baton he carried, barked out,

"Nominative, vocative and accusative. Genitive, dative, ablative. Right with me. Amo, amas, amat amamas amatis amant. Repeat!"

He strode around the room, gown flowing out behind him, cocking an ear at everyone to make sure they were chanting.

"Speak up, boy, I can't hear you," he exhorted.

I was never very good at Latin, but I can certainly remember that first lesson. It also surprised me what valuable words and derivations have remained with me over the next sixty years.

Another teacher who made an impression on me that first day was Mr Young, the Deputy Head, who taught geography. Laugh a minute was Mr Young.

"I'm Young", he offered, tittering at his joke as he was clearly approaching ninety.

He was another who wanted to get on with things, slinging out textbooks with indecent haste before firing out questions about capital cities to warm us up.

"Venezuela?" he offered.

Pregnant pause.

"It's Crackers", he chortled, pleased with his pathetic wordplay on the South American country's Caracas.

Funny old chap, Mr Young, but geography was to become my favourite subject.

We broke for lunch where there were two sittings which we had been told about earlier. You either went straight to lunch at the bell or played football in the yard and queued up for food half an hour later.

The food quality pleasantly surprised me - it was not bad at all, although the portions were a little on the small size.

The afternoon went smoothly enough, and I remember meeting the gruff Mr Sargent, the French teacher, and the RE teacher, Mr Wilson. He introduced himself.

"Good afternoon, 1A. I am Mr Wilson. You will learn my nickname soon enough from the others. I am Bogger Wilson. Bogger, the bugger from Burton. That's me."

His language surprised me and took me aback. An RE teacher swearing in class! And he used the word that had caused me to be grounded several years previously.

Four o'clock and the end of the school day came around quickly. The bus journey back home was much more chatty than on the way in, with pupils, particularly the new first years, discussing their impressions of the day.

On the short walk up the hill towards home, I debated how I would explain the satchel incident. Dad would not be home, so I would have to speak to Mum. There was no way I could hide the fact of its mutilation, so I would confront the situation head-on.

I opened the back door and breezily shouted,

"Hi Mum, I'm back."

"Oh! How did you get on?"

"Great,"

"Yeah, I met up with Keith and Alan, who decided they should customise my satchel, so I didn't look like a first-year."

"What do you mean?"

"Well, look."

"Oh, John! John, what have they done?"

Understandably, she was not happy, but I explained and calmed her down. She liked both Keith and Alan, so that helped.

"It cost a lot of money. Now, look at it. It is a mess." She continued quietly.

Not covering things up was the right approach, as she seemed to accept the situation after a few minutes. The important thing was that when Mum told him about it later, Dad did not make an issue of it at all, probably thinking,

Boys will be boys.

The rest of the week was a whirlwind of introductions to previously unheard-of subjects, like chemistry, physics and technical drawing. There were more different teachers and classrooms. We also started the day in the hall with a whole school assembly. The Head addressed us all and there were readings and hymns.

We had games one day and PE another, so I met the PE Master, Mr Smith. He was only in his twenties, and he wore a tracksuit, was fit-looking and enthusiastic, and I looked up to him from the outset. In games, we had football, where he cast his eyes over the potential talent and likely prospects for his under-13 team, drawn from the first two year groups, about which he had told us.

Playground football games were very popular, with about twenty-a-side playing at break and dinner time across the entire width of the playground. We would play with a tennis ball, as the rules did not allow a full-size ball because of the pitch being surrounded by windows.

With so many players, and using such a tiny ball made making an impact tricky; I continued to work hard on my skills and enjoyed taking on the older boys.

Over a few weeks, we first formers became used to Thomas Alleyne's systems and procedures and quickly bedded down into a routine. School assembly, lessons, football at break and dinnertime, more lessons, the four o'clock bell and back home became the daily pattern.

Many boys were local, from the town of Uttoxeter, so could walk home. However, for us bus travellers, who lived out in the sticks, the journey between school and home again became quite a social event and often a good laugh.

I remember racing into technical drawing early in the term, which was the first lesson after lunch. Hot and sweaty, and my hands dirty from playing football, I had not given myself sufficient time to clean up or prepare. Also, as I quickly realised, I only had a stubby, blunt HB pencil when we had always been told to have a sharp 2H pencil ready for action.

Mr Ivinghoe was less than impressed, and after balling me out at length, I felt quite uncomfortable. It seemed the incident had doomed our relationship from the outset. I would never be the next Isambard Kingdom Brunel in his (or my) eyes. Designing and drawing ships, railways and bridges would not be my forte, and our relationship from that moment on was never the best. To be fair, though, there seemed to be only three or four boys in the class who produced work of a high enough standard to please him. Old Ivanhoe, our nickname for him from the television series, just focused on them, ignoring the pathetic efforts of the rest of us. At the end of the year, most of the class came about 7th equal, which to me was pretty acceptable.

CHAPTER 7

MAKING THE TEAM

A few weeks into term, Mr Smith posted up some trial teams for the U13 squad, and he picked me in one at right half, which I found an exciting prospect.

He had planned the tryouts for after school one evening the following week, and I had to tell Mum I would be late home. Mr Smith refereed, kept his eye on players and moved boys around a bit to try different formations. A couple of other teachers were helping on the sidelines, marking points down on clipboards. I thought I had played ok and made a point of checking the noticeboard for the rest of the week.

There was a sports team bulletin board in the main entrance hall, which became a focal point for me. It delighted me when, on Friday, Mr Smith put the team sheet up, and the U13 team included me in the right half position.

My friend from Cheadle, Michael, was inside me at centre half while two cousins in my class, Nick and Rob Millington, were in the forward line.

We were down to play a school at Etwall in eight days. The place was located fifteen miles along the A50, close to Derby. We were to have a practice session the following Wednesday after school. This was it. What I had been waiting for.

The practice seemed to go relatively smoothly, and we were all looking forward to the match. There were only four first-years picked as most of the team were older and bigger second-formers, but we fitted in well, I thought.

With after-school training sessions, the problem was that by the time I was ready to get the public bus home, I was starving hungry. I would have to stop at a shop and get a Mars bar to gulp down just to keep me going. This hunger became an enduring problem as the school meal portions were on the stingy side. I remember once waiting for the bus after a late practice session when I bought and devoured a whole Swiss Roll to satisfy my hunger pangs.

The Saturday of the game came around, and I was up early to clean and polish my boots and pack my freshly laundered shorts, socks, and a towel in my kit bag. I then had to get the public bus, showing my school travel card, to Uttoxeter, before meeting up and going on a coach to Etwall.

Getting changed, I could feel the frisson of excitement amongst the team. Mr Smith came in to give us a bit of a pep talk, and then we trotted out on the pitch, ready to do battle.

It was a tight game, and we played well, taking the lead just before halftime. But Etwall were a good team and fought back vigorously to score two goals in the second period to edge us out. The result was a disappointment, but I still loved the whole occasion.

We probably played half a dozen times that season, in the end winning more than we lost. I can still clearly remember the whole routine of cleaning my boots, packing my kit, travelling on the bus and then playing the games. My game developed into that of being a solid tackling midfielder, keen to provide the forward line with valuable possession and not waste any ball.

That autumn also introduced me to the game of fives. There were two main variations of the game, promoted by Eton and Rugby schools. Our court, with a step and a buttress, was the Eton variant. There was an open practice session organised one evening after school for pupils to try the game out, and I was keen to have a go.

It is a simple game where players hit something like a golf ball but covered in soft leather, with a gloved hand against a wall. It is like squash (without a racket, obviously) or hand pelota.

I took to it straight away and thoroughly enjoyed it. I ended up playing so frequently, mainly playing against much older boys, that, like other regulars, I dispensed with the use of a glove. My hand became hard and calloused so that it could withstand the whacking of a hard ball. It was a game I would get better at and enjoy throughout my time at Uttoxeter Grammar.

Another young lad my age, Patrick, was also becoming good at the game, and we often played and practiced together.

Unfortunately for us, one of the older boys, a sixth former and probably eighteen, took a shine to us and separately persuaded us to go with him on some pretext or other up to a room in the oldest part of the school for which he had a key. I did not know what was to happen, being entirely innocent of these things.

Having taken me up to his secret room and gained my confidence, I suppose, he then put his hand down my trousers and into my pants and began 'fiddling about'. I was most uncomfortable and shocked about this, so he stopped, but then undid his flies and masturbated until he ejaculated across the room. He then got himself straight, and we left the room as if nothing had happened.

I was very shocked and horrified at this behaviour and clarified that I would keep well away from him from then on. I did not tell anyone about this unsavoury episode but did chat with Patrick as I had some sort of inclination that the same thing had happened to him. In much the same way, he confirmed it had, and we both concluded we would give him a wide berth in the future. Beyond that, we told no one.

In late October, we had a surprise visit to Cheadle from Uncle Arthur, one of Dad's older brothers. He had been the first of the family to move away from Boston, living just outside Bristol with his wife, Auntie Millicent. They had no children. Later, the story I heard from Mum was that Auntie Millicent declared that if she were over thirty, by the time her husband came home from the war, she would not have children.

Uncle Arthur seemed to have done well in business. He was an independent sales agent and represented several manufacturers in the sweets and confectionery industry, as well as the Danish company Plumrose, which produced processed ham products and a wide range of other household names. He had ample stocks of samples of products, and on this occasion, he brought us quite a few enormous tins of ham and other preserved meats and an abundance of Barratt's and Swizzels's branded sweets, sherbet dabs and liquorice for us boys.

On this visit, as he seemed to have a contract with a fireworks manufacturer, he also turned up with a massive supply of commercial-sized pyrotechnics. These large-scale rockets, roman candles and firecrackers dwarfed the size of the typical shop-bought selection boxes. We were all excited and surprised at what a show could be in prospect.

Once Uncle Arthur had left, excited 'thank yous' ringing in his ears, we bombarded Dad with demanded questions about inviting friends around for the best bonfire party ever. He did not need much persuading. Mum and Dad were up for hosting such an event, and we put plans in motion. We invited all the usual gang along with their parents.

We had everything organised by November the fifth. In those days, there would be no way we could set any fireworks off before the proper day. We had built and lit an enormous bonfire in the garden, and Mum had done a mountain of baking. She was also in charge of cooking sausages and burgers and preparing some salads and other accompaniments. Some of the other mums helped as well.

Dad was the fireworks supremo, not allowing anyone else near the stocks, except Frank from next door, who was the designated safety officer. We all watched in awe as a spectacularly colourful, crashing, and crackling exhibition illuminated the clear night sky. To multiple oohs, aahs and wows, the display continued for what seemed like forever, with everyone enjoying what they were all in agreement about. It was the best Guy Fawkes' night ever. My brothers and I basked in the family's reflected glory, of putting on such a great show thanks to Uncle Arthur.

The fireworks party certainly did the family's street credibility no harm at all - the Stanilands certainly knew how to put on a party was the consensus.

So, wishing to strike while the iron was hot and with Christmas racing upon us quickly, we boys then pestered Mum and Dad to allow us to host a Christmas party for all our friends. They seemed to enjoy having a houseful and were excellent hosts. We easily persuaded them that this was a sound idea. We set the date for a few days after Boxing Day but still in the school holiday period. Dad was too busy working in the run-up to Christmas to stage the event then.

We had quite a house full of youngsters, with Dad as the party organiser and Mum as head of catering. While some of the older teens would have perhaps hoped for a no-adult party, the consensus was that Mum and Dad were good fun and in no way fuddy-duddies. Or in the day's parlance 'squares', so the party would be excellent.

Dad resurrected some of his old party games like Nelson's Eye and Submarines, which went down well, causing much hilarity, and invented a new one which proved a hit. He devised a racing car game where he had drawn out a track on the reverse of an old roll of wallpaper with about 30 stages from the start to the chequered flag. There were six cars in the race, in their designated lanes. Each faced a variety of hazards at different points on the track such as 'oil on the track, miss a turn' or 'spun off go back three places': or some sped up progress like 'excellent manoeuvre advance two places' or 'late-braking advance one'. It was a simple dice game requiring a throw of a six to start and then taking turns to throw to progress down the track. We boys provided the cars from our vast collection in the playroom.

Dad also ran the book where we could bet a few pennies on the race outcome. The gambling element seemed immensely grown-up, and the game held our keen attention for many rounds.

After a break to tackle the enormous spread of food and fizzy drinks Mum had laid out on the extended dining room table, it was back to the lounge for more games.

A few rounds of the classic postman's knock went down well. Keith and Alan were very keen to get on the other side of the door. Especially when Jill, last year's Carnival Queen, who had become part of the gang, was the one calling out the number.

Continuing the post office theme, then Dad had another postally orientated bit of fun lined up. The game involved dividing into boys' and girls' teams and charging around the entire house with 'letters' requiring to be posted in specific locations he had made to look like red pillar boxes. He placed these strategically around the house. Everyone raced around the house, causing chaos and hilarity.

The highlight game was probably 'murder in the dark', whereby Dad dealt playing cards discreetly to everyone, with one particular queen designating the murderer and another the detective. The holders of those were to keep their identities secret.

Then, all but the detective left the room and could go anywhere in the darkened house. After some time, the murderer, when they had selected their victim, would then grab that person lightly around the neck. The poor innocent would scream loudly after a few seconds to allow the perpetrator a little time to escape. They would then put the lights on, and people were supposed to stay where they were. The detective would then begin their enquiries and hopefully solve the murder.

This scenario led to a load of boys and girls, many in their mid-teens, like Keith and Alan, the Whitefields and the Staniers, charging around a darkened house. People were diving under beds, into cupboards, hiding in wardrobes, and taking advantage of the situation for illicit fumblings and smooches. Great fun all around was the agreed conclusion.

Soon after the party, we had a decent fall of snow, so we spent the last few days of the Christmas break sledging all day. Up the Leek road about a mile and over to the west was a hilly area of rough common land, which we selected for our track. We groomed the piste, using a shovel borrowed from home, and added piles of fresh snow where it was sparse to create our version of the Cresta Run. The course was probably about half a mile long, starting steeply, and then the final run-in flattened out a little. A barbed-wire fence marked the edge of a farmer's meadow here. A few yards into the field was a pond that was frozen over and covered in snow.

Once we had packed down the track by regular use and it was running faster, it became possible to race under the fence and finish up halfway across the pond. We needed to be careful to avoid being decapitated by barbed wire and to double-check that the ice would hold up.

The mathematicians in the group (the older lads) decided it would be a good idea to time our runs. So we had a measured area of the track where we could put the stopwatch on the entry and exit points and thus work out our speed. We had the equipment and had a section of forty-four yards measured out. We chose the distance as we knew that forty-four feet per second was the equivalent of 30mph. From that point, it was easy to calculate our speed as three seconds for the distance would show a speed of 30mph. We were frequently reaching rates higher than that, with the record being about 40mph.

Because dusk fell not long after four o'clock, we had to pack up sledging in this location around that time, but we had another early evening venue lined up. Just up a couple of hundred yards from our house, Highfield Road curved downhill steeply from Leek Road, and the streetlights meant we had enough illumination to toboggan down the excellent slope.

There were few car owners down the road in that era and any that came home were happy to park at the top and allow us our fun. Two or three girls who had been at junior school with me joined one time. Susie Rylance, I particularly recalled, was a pretty, dark-haired girl who I think seemed to like me. I remember me and Susie teaming up and her laying on top of me as we sped down the course. At the bottom of the hill, the road curved sharply to the right, and, really whizzing with the additional weight, I failed to take the bend properly and crashed into a pile of snow. We were in a laughing heap covered in snow and faces just inches apart; we simultaneously moved in to kiss. Quite a memorable sledging day, that one.

Back at school after the New Year, it was more of the same. As the year's first edition of The Beano pointed out, the year appeared the same when it was upside down, 1961.

As far as it concerned me, everything was ticking along ok academically, and I felt I was progressing reasonably in most subjects. I got an idea of my standing in class when the teachers tested us. I was not one of the class swots (or cloggers, as we referred to them) like Thomas, the head's son, and half a dozen others. Michael, who was at the Cheadle School with me, also seemed to perform well academically, and I probably fell in just below that grouping.

I was still rubbish at Tech Drawing, but as the teacher had almost given up with the bulk of the class, I just accepted that. I was not much cop at woodwork either, taking a term to make a tool for pricking out plants. This exercise, showing my ability to make a mortise and tenon joint, he deemed to be only worthy of a six out of ten. It deserved better.

I was also having a bit of trouble with French, as we were being taught some sort of phonetic method with 44 distinct sounds or phonemes. I ultimately failed to grasp the concepts involved. Dad didn't have any experience with it, either, when I asked him about it.

"This is not proper French, John" was his sole, frustrated comment.

So I just muddled along as best I could.

My main point of focus was outside of the classroom, though. It was football in the playground, football practice and matches (house games and school fixtures), playing friendly fives matches, and playing in the house competition and cross-country running. The latter I had quite taken to and used to go on training runs two or three times a week. I was in the junior and intermediate teams, and we would have occasional races against other schools in the area.

In March of that year, I ran for the school at a big inter-school competition on Cannock Chase in the county's south. I clearly remember the day, freezing cold and quite windy, less for the race, which I did alright at considering the enormous field and age range of the competitors, but more because it was the day Nicolaus Silver won the Grand National. According to a snippet of conversation I picked up while boarding the bus, the horse was the first grey to win the big race that century. I don't know why, as I didn't have then, and never had since any interest in horse racing, but the fact has stuck with me.

That Spring, the music teacher also chose me for the school choir. We would perform Handel's Messiah shortly. I was not familiar with this sort of music but became very impressed with the sound we could produce with a full choir, a Capella, ranging from the boy sopranos (boys in my age group) through tenors, baritones and the basses with some of the sixth formers alongside a few teachers.

All the different voices coming together and sections singing separate parts occasionally, I found almost magical. I can still clearly remember belting out the Hallelujah chorus and thoroughly enjoying it.

'For the Lord God, omnipotent reigneth. Hallelujah! Hallelujah! Hallelujah! Hallelujah!'

We had quite a few practice sessions, and the music teacher, a dapper little moustachioed man who spoke in a clipped, precise manner, was a real stickler for perfection. We performed over three nights for an audience of local dignitaries and parents as far as I can recall. I remember we received several standing ovations, so the full house appreciated our efforts.

I also had to perform that year at our chapel, as I was the narrator of the Easter Story that we presented to the congregation. The big story of that occasion, however, was my youngest brother, who was too young to play an active part but was sitting up on the stage area with the rest of the Sunday School pupils. He spent the whole time trying to blow out one of the large candles that were some way to his left. He would blow, the candle would flicker ominously to the point of dying out entirely and then, in a split second, reignite. The congregation decided this little drama was more worthy of their attention than my pronouncements. But I found the episode a distraction and had to focus completely on not messing up my narration. Silly idiot. I could kill him.

He repeated his blowing on more than several occasions with the same result until he gave up out of boredom, and the congregation could reconnect with my Easter message.

***

Dad and I were still going to water polo at Hanley. I was by now getting more involved in the practices and picking up some valuable skills. I seemed to take to the game readily and could not wait until I was good enough to play in actual matches.

The summer term meant an introduction to athletics and cricket in games lessons. I was more interested in the former than the latter and practised starts, hurdling and improving my long jump technique rather than bowling off-breaks and perfecting cover drives. I don't know why I didn't particularly take to cricket, perhaps that Mr Smith was more an athlete than a cricketer and that Dad had never played the game, except on the beach.

That May, our rural bus route gang, enjoyed some sort of reflected glory as the railway line we crossed at Rocester every day was the first in the country to have an automatic barrier installed. The new system involved flashing lights and bells to signal an approaching train and a barrier falling into place to block just the left-hand side of the road. The new installation made the national television news, with a film clip showing our actual crossing. I remember pointing it out excitedly to Mum and Dad. Quite an important event for a twelve-year-old.

The climax of the summer term was Sports Day, a memorable day in the school's calendar, and parents all came along to watch the spectacle. Some events took place before the big day, and I had picked up a couple of seconds in the cross-country and the long jump. As a first-year boy competing against the older second-formers, this was not too bad.

I knew I was in with a shout in the 80 yards, 220 yards and 440 yards on the day itself, although I had one particularly powerful and tall, long-legged opponent with whom to contend. He proved too good for me, and I had to settle for three second places, just edged out in the shortest sprint by a whisker. However, this augured well for the following year, when my nemesis would become an intermediate contender, leaving the junior field clear for me. I also noticed that he was wearing spikes, so I determined I would get some for next season.

Better, warmer summer weather brought out a feature of school behaviour that was new to me. Uttoxeter Girl's High School was on a site next to our establishment. Our playing fields shared the same extensive plot of land, with no physical separation but a grassed slope running for about a hundred yards beyond the lovely little wooden cricket pavilion. The school groundsman had marked a white line at the top of the slight hill denoting the edge of the Grammar school's pitches and one at the bottom to designate the boundary of the girls' territory. They considered the three-metre space in between the lines as '*no-man's-land*', with heavy sanctions applied for anyone seen entering from either school. It was possible, just about, to have a shouted conversation between the schools and a lot of the older boys and girls engaged in flirtatious chats, lying prone right at the relevant boundary line.

The other event lodged in my mind that summer was that the Australian Cricket team was touring and playing test matches against England. Although not really into cricket from a playing perspective, I immediately detected the significance of an 'Ashes' series and followed the five test matches as much as possible, listening on the radio at home or else on my newly gained small transistor radio.

The visitors won the five-match series 2-1 with two drawn games. There were names from both sides who were, and still are, giants of the game. England had all-time greats Trueman, Statham and Lock on the bowling front and May, Compton, Barrington and Dexter amongst the batsmen. The Australian tourists, under Richie Benaud, had Alan Davidson, Wally Grout, Neil Harvey, and Bill Lawry in their ranks.

Quite a few classmates also followed the series, and cricket became the trend for a time. There was a minor craze going around to play 'Owzat' surreptitiously in class. There was a proper game marketed with little metal hexagons thrown to determine whether the player had scored a single, a boundary, or if it was a dot ball. The possibility of an appeal was also there. When the appeal came along, the player rolled a second piece to show 'not out' or 'how out'. Most of us just improvised using suitable bits of an appropriately hexagonal-shaped pencil. We filled in dozens of pages of our rough books with cricket scores, using the names of the Australian and English players. It was great for adding a bit of interest to a boring lesson, although one had to be discrete to avoid being spotted.

At the end of my first year at Thomas Alleyne's, we had examinations in all academic subjects with marks awarded towards our overall position in the form. Happy that I had done my best, I was content, if a little disappointed not to have achieved a couple of places higher. Placing 11th out of 33, I ended up going home clutching a decent enough report with no black marks and a lot of praise from WNS, the PE teacher.

The summer holidays spread out before us that July, and it was a programme of playing football down at the rec, going off with the gang up to Hawksmoor or enjoying family picnics at the weekend. The potential money-making circuit of the village fetes was in prospect. I was, after all, a professional sprinter. And something new for this year was a Sunday school train trip to that mecca of northern seaside resorts, Blackpool.

Dad largely organised this outing, and we had an early morning start, excitedly taking our places on board and immediately ripping into the goodie bags we had been given. For most of us, this was a very rare expedition by rail.

In Blackpool, we went on to the beach, and Dad organised a mass cricket game before we all explored the delights of the piers, the promenade and the Pleasure Gardens. There was the scary new roller coaster ride, the Wild Mouse, which I found quite nerve-wracking. I had already been on this the previous year with Margaret, our next-door neighbour. I was not really overkeen on repeating the experience, but there was considerable peer pressure to do so.

After fish and chips all around, and a trip by tram to see the illuminations, we made it back to the station for the long journey back, most falling into an exhausted sleep. At least I got to see the spectacular light displays this time around.

Dad was also the prime mover that summer in staging a day out for Post Office friends and family under the auspices of the Stoke-on-Trent Post Office Sports and Social Club, with whom we still took part in the weekly family swimming sessions at Burslem. With our exploration of the surrounding countryside over the last couple of years, Dad knew where he wanted to stage his 'Family Fun Day'. It was in a sizeable flattish field high above the steep wooded slopes running down to the River Churnet.

On the opposite side of the valley were the highly acclaimed gardens of Alton Towers (this was a few years before the development of the location as a major theme park with many sophisticated roller-coaster-type rides for thrill-seekers). It was a far more genteel venue at this time, with vast acreages of beautiful gardens which attracted lots of promenading pensioners.

Dad had to negotiate the use of the field with the farmer, who was quite agreeable when he explained the plans to him. It was mutually beneficial, as he was to provide eggs, bacon, sausages and milk, which we would need for the mass catering planned. He could also provide toilet facilities. These were in the form of an ancient but clean, outside three-seater wooden thunderbox set up, which caused much hilarity when first encountered by visitors when the day came around.

It was quite a major logistical exercise for Dad and his committee of helpers to pull off, but a wonderful sunny summer's day of food, drink, music, laughter, and games was a significant success. I felt very proud of Dad and the organisational skills, hard work and enthusiasm he showed to pull off such a successful event. Mum also worked hard giving moral support and baking mountains of cakes, pies, and desserts, leading a team of other wives and girlfriends in the catering department.

We put our large ex-army ridge tent to use, and other family tents commandeered from friends as the food tent, bar or tea room. The tents would also provide shelter if the weather proved inclement. Luckily, the weather, however, was beautiful all day.

A treasure hunt trailing through the woodlands on the valley sides was very successful, with participants looking for coloured cards that Dad and I had partially hidden in strategic spots a few hours earlier.

The grand finale, though, was a tip-it-and-run knock-out cricket tournament involving about a dozen teams playing for the trophy of a large chamber pot painted with an appropriate inscription. This involved everyone, and there was much merriment and good-natured competitiveness.

We were off to Anglesey at the end of July for our usual two weeks, and this time, on most of our beach excursions, we took Mr Jones' daughter, Madge, about my age, and her younger cousin, a boy, called Rhydian who literally could not speak a word of English. Madge had to translate to and from Welsh all day. In Anglesey, where every second person was called Jones, this was quite the norm and a lot of the older generation, like Madge's father, never got to grips with communicating in the language of the people from the East.

CHAPTER 8

A SECOND FORMER NOW

September came around, and it seemed a little strange going back to school as a second former, and so not quite at the bottom of the school pecking order. This time we had the freshers to look down on.

Our home classroom was now in the school's major block of accommodation, and our desks were the old-fashioned iron-framed units with bench seats built-in and set on tiered platforms. We still sat alphabetically, and we had a fresh addition to our class, who sat immediately behind me. His name was Iain (which I thought was a funny way of spelling Ian) Sutherland. I introduced myself to him and tried to chat, but he had a very thick accent that I had difficulty understanding. I eventually worked out he had come down from a fishing town on the East coast of Scotland called Peterhead, or 'Peterheeed' as he called it. Careful listening over time and slight modifications made on his part to the way he spoke meant we could rub along quite nicely.

We were now considered responsible enough to use ink pens, and the teachers gave out plain wooden instruments with a nib at the end and a small supply of blotting paper. One class member became an ink monitor and had the job of keeping ink wells filled from a large container stored at the front of the class.

Fingers, shirts, texts and exercise books received more than their fair share of splodges, and some boys (never me, of course) used to fire pellets, using ink-soaked blotting paper, around the class when the teacher turned his back.

Soon into the new term, we set off on the school bus from Cheadle as usual on a particularly blowy day. As we approached the steeply wooded areas around Alton and Oakamoor, we realised we were in the middle of a major storm. We spotted scores of trees that the powerful gusts had brought down.

We did not know, but we were experiencing the tail end of Hurricane Debbie, an immense force of nature coming from across the Atlantic, having caused severe devastation on the American side of the world first. It had blown down and uprooted vast numbers of trees and caused massive structural damage all over the country. Gusts exceeded 100mph, we heard later. The bus driver could get around some of the earlier hazards, but there were several sections where we had to wait for workers to clear massive tree trunks out of the road with tractors and chainsaws. These delays meant we were over two hours late for school. It was all tremendously exciting.

Later that day, we were in a lesson in one of the Portakabin classrooms when suddenly a loud whooshing sound, followed by a tremendous crash, had us all looking out of the windows. The hurricane blew the whole of the dining hall roof, a section of sixty-foot off the rest of the building, and sent it clattering down in the middle of the playground - quite a spectacle and potentially so dangerous. We had to stay the whole day indoors and not change classrooms like we usually would, as roof slates, trees, large branches, and even chimney pots were thundering down at regular intervals.

Thankfully, the winds had died down by the time we took the bus home, so we had a clear run, although there were many examples of the devastation caused by the hurricane with damage to houses, fences, brick walls and, of course, vast amounts of trees down all along the route.

A few weeks later, another natural occurrence was in the news and piqued my curiosity. A massive volcanic eruption occurred in Tristão da Cunha, a British Protectorate, a speck in the South Atlantic and the world's most remote inhabited archipelago. This event forced the entire population of some two hundred and sixty-four residents to be evacuated to the UK. After being housed at an old RAF camp at Calshot on the Solent, they eventually returned home in 1963, so it was quite a lengthy stay in the UK for them. I remember using my school atlas to work out exactly where the place was and being amazed at how far away from absolutely everywhere it was.

Paul, a junior employee and protégé of dad at the Post Office and his fiancée Pauline, around this time, often came to babysit for us when Mum and Dad went off to some social function or other. As they were more mature than some of our teenage babysitters, they were a little stricter about bedtimes, but I could stay up an hour after they had packed my brothers off to bed. I could not outstay my welcome as they understandably wanted some time on their own, which I appreciated, but I got on well with them both and particularly enjoyed chatting with Paul about football. He was an avid Stoke City fan, and that autumn the big news was the return of the 46-year-old Stanley Matthews to his Stoke roots.

The *'wizard of dribble'* as he was known in the sports press, a longtime star of England and an FA Cup winner with Blackpool in the 1953 final, the match remembered henceforward as '*The Matthews Final',* was a true legend of the game. He was European Footballer of the Year in 1956 and was the only player to be knighted whilst still playing the game in that same year. He kept himself in such good shape that he could play at the top level until he was over 50. Paul said he would take me to a match to see him play if I would like, and of course, I jumped at the chance.

I clearly remember being on the densely packed and noisy terraces at the Victoria Ground close to the action. I was on Matthews' right wing when the diminutive number seven, in his red and white striped shirt and baggy white shorts, bamboozled the fullback with some mazy footwork, cut in, and with the cross being expected by players and spectators alike just lashed it past the goalkeeper and into the net. There was a joyful uproar as the crowd celebrated the moment, almost disbelieving the mercurial skills on display. It was the 25th of November 1961, and Stoke City beat Newcastle United 3-1. Since that day, I have been a Stoke supporter, admittedly from a distance, but I always look out for their results and follow the team's normally stuttering progress.

***

Christmas came around once again, and I don't remember exactly if we visited relatives in Boston over the holiday period or not. I think we may have gone, but it would have just been a 'there and back in a day' visit.

We boys always found the day trip, which we undertook occasionally, tedious as the journey took a good three hours each way by car. When we got there, we went to various relatives' homes, sitting and getting bored while the adults sipped endless cups of tea or coffee and chatted about (to my mind) inanities. At Grandma's, the conversation was quite depressing.

"Remember Mrs Coates at number 31?"

"Yes."

"She's dead."

"Old Albert, you know, the butcher's brother, he died the other week. Heart."

The only good thing about these excursions was that we could usually pocket some cash. Relatives used to slip us all a two bob bit (10p) or half a crown (12p), and Mrs Reece, a lovely lady who lived next door to Grandma, always gave us thirty old pennies (12p) each which she had saved especially for our visits. This weighed a ton, but we were not complaining.

Mr Reece, who never moved from his fireside chair, just grunted in acknowledgement of our presence while his kindly wife fussed around us, doling out sweets or biscuits before presenting the hoard of copper coins. Stinking of tobacco smoke, the old chap seemed to spend his entire life sat smoking, cleaning out one or other of his vast array of pipes from his elaborate rack, or refilling a bowl with Old London Shag or whatever.

Once familial duties were over, we were all grateful when we headed back home. Mum and Dad were, I feel, pleased to return to our cosy home, lifestyle and circle of friends in Cheadle.

It was funny, but none of the Boston family ever visited us at Cheadle, except Grandma and Nana and Grandad, whom Dad had to drive over and collect. I picked up from Mum that it disappointed Dad that his relationship with his youngest brother, David, had become so much more distant than it once had been. When younger, they were close buddies with a shared passion for sport, but the responsibilities of marriage, family and careers, together with the physical distance between the respective homes since our move from Lincolnshire, had inevitably affected the close fraternal connection they once enjoyed.

Three of Dad's siblings and their families, who had moved away from Boston, visited from time to time, though, and we occasionally got to see four of our girl cousins. Just before Christmas, Uncle Arthur again diverted from one of his business trips to pop around, bringing a considerable supply of sweets that would last the whole of the next term.

Speaking of Uncle Arthur, he was always very generous with Christmas presents. That year, I received a beautiful Conway Stewart fountain pen from him and Aunt Millicent, which I was sure would help me improve my handwriting. I could now abandon the pathetic instruments the school handed out and made a promise to myself to write more neatly and avoid blots in the future.

The typical pattern of family life continued after Christmas and into January 1962. In the new year, Dad's workload was a little less frantic. Mum did not have to bake huge batches of mince pies for hungry postal workers and we boys quickly settled back into the school routine.

I seemed to get more homework daily, meaning I had to escape upstairs immediately after tea and focus hard for an hour or two on my studies. In my single bedroom, where I had a desk and chair under the window, I was wrestling with Latin conjugations or chemical formulae in my own little world. It could sometimes be a pain and a bit frustrating, but I took it in my stride. I could see my brothers thought little of the idea of homework. They could go straight to the front room and play with their new Christmas toys for a couple of hours.

With homework, going to Hanley with Dad for water polo practice and watching him play matches, staying behind late at school a couple of nights for fives or house football matches I did not seem to have a spare moment, but I liked the non-stop action.

I was also playing for the school U 13s on Saturdays regularly. While I was an 'ever-present' at either right or left half, I still always felt the excitement on Thursday lunchtime as I went to the noticeboard to check whether the team sheet was up on the board. It was invariably there; My name was on the team sheet in neat handwriting and signed off by WNS.

I also still enjoyed the pre-match ritual of Saturday morning breakfast, getting my kit ready before walking down the hill to catch a bus to Uttoxeter. We were winning most matches, and I enjoyed playing immensely. My game still involved continuous running and tackling, but I was now making more than the odd foray into the attack to smash in a goal or two.

As I was becoming older and perhaps more mature, I took more interest in current affairs and what was happening in the world around me, watching the television news regularly.

A lead story that January was the trial of James Hanratty, who brutally murdered Michael Gregsten and raped and shot Valerie Storey, Gregsten's mistress, leaving her paralysed from the neck down. He committed the egregious crime in a layby just off the A6 in Bedfordshire, and henceforth, the media referred to the case as the A6 murder. The jury found Hanratty guilty and handed down a capital sentence. He was one of the last people in the country to be hanged.

I remember the case clearly and fully appreciated that Hanratty was evil and deserved to be punished by life imprisonment. However, I could not see capital punishment as anything other than brutal, degrading, and inappropriate in modern democratic society.

***

One day, just after half-term, I missed my morning school bus. There were no alternatives available, but I then suddenly had a brainwave. A company bus left Cheadle every weekday to take local women employees to Elke's, the biscuit manufacturer in Uttoxeter. I plucked up the courage to speak to the driver and explain my predicament, and he readily agreed he could take me. I then had to face a wave of barracking, cackling, and ribald mickey-taking from a bus full of young and middle-aged female biscuit makers. Quite humiliating, but I got to school on time.

That Easter, we took the long trip up to Harrogate to spend a few days with my Mum's relatives, Auntie Clarice, whom Mum was named after, and Uncle Frank. They were a childless couple in their seventies who seemed to live a very simple and frugal life. Their daily routine comprised a morning walk after breakfast, reading the paper and doing the crossword during the day (Uncle Frank) or busying herself with needlework, cooking and cleaning (Auntie Clarice) and then playing whist in the evenings. They didn't have a television.

"Waste of time", pronounced the curmudgeonly Uncle Frank.

Mum and Dad took them out to various scenic sites, of which there is a large number in North Yorkshire for walks and a little picnic. The family also explored Knaresborough and took a rowing boat out on the River Nidd, which I remember well as Dad allowed me to take the oars.

We still had time to explore Harrogate itself. I have always thought the town to be a most delightful place, with some solid, handsome Victorian buildings and wonderful, immaculately maintained parks and gardens. There was also the vast open common land of 'The Stray'. As it often can be at Easter, the weather was hailstorms and driving rain one minute and blue skies and sunshine the next, but we dodged the worst of it and even fitted in a round of pitch and putt golf.

In the evenings, we all ended up playing cards after Auntie Clarice and Mum had produced an evening meal for us all. It was the first time they introduced me to scallops, made from deep-fried battered potato slices, and we boys thought they were great.

Uncle Frank was to put it politely, a churlish grumbler. If, as I did frequently, I beat him at cards; it was always,

"Eh, mugs for luck." Or "Anyun can win if you get t'cards." He met one of my efforts of pleading that I had won fair and square and, with a certain amount of skill, with derision and a theatrical snort. After that, I decided it would be politic to keep my counsel and not try to argue the toss.

Uncle Frank would also regularly come out with some homespun Yorkshire philosophy proposing that "If thi does owt for nowt allus do it fer thi sen." Or "'ear all, see all, say nowt, eat all, sup all, pay nowt," and concerning the notoriously cold and fickle weather up in Yorkshire, "n'e'r cast a clout afore May is out", advising to keep wearing a vest until June. And one phrase he aimed at me frequently in a mildly derogatory manner: "Gi o'er ya daft happath."

Halfway up Harlow Hill, about a mile out of town, their house was a large, handsome, stone-terraced property with an attic and a cellar, so it had plenty of space. I had my bedroom at the front of the property, next to a grandfather clock on the landing. The ticking was so loud it kept me awake long into the night, but the clanging chime every hour was quite something else, often rousing me from a deep sleep when I had eventually dropped off.

We followed that trip away with another weekend break a month later when we went to Uncle Eric and Auntie Doff's (Dorothy was her given name, and she was Dad's sister) in Luton. Uncle Eric managed a gent's outfitters, with extensive rambling living accommodation at the back and above the shop premises.

We got on well with Julie, my middle brother's age, chatting and playing records. She had quite a collection of hit singles, and we played them constantly on her dad's impressive new stereophonic radiogram. Dion's 'The Wanderer' was a favourite, with songs of other American stars like Bobby Darin, Bobby Vee, Chris Montez and Del Shannon getting plays. Cliff Richard and the Shadows had also had a big hit with 'The Young Ones', so we gave that disc a few spins. Probably too many for uncle Eric at one stage.

"Julie, give that flipping rubbish a bit of a break; let me put some proper music on. Here George, have a listen to this," he continued before slotting on the LP of Tchaikovsky's 1812 Overture, turning the sound up to full.

I did not know what stereo music was, and I don't think Dad did either, but when cannons, bells and fireworks thundered on both sides of the room, we got a pretty good idea.

Later that weekend, we walked on Ivinghoe Beacon, a prominent and high hill in the Chilterns and had a picnic whilst watching gliders soaring high above. We also visited the Whipsnade zoological park.

I loved Whipsnade as, as far as possible, the animals had free rein to roam around spacious enclosures and were not in awfully constricting cages like the London Zoo I had heard about. I had visited London Zoo and have seen photos of me there, but do not remember it. It was lovely at Whipsnade when tiny and very cute baby deer would approach shyly for food, but young wallabies would boldly bound up and take snacks directly from your hand.

CHAPTER 9

JUNIOR VICTOR LUDORUM

In the summer term, football being over, I focused on athletics, although I was still playing fives, an all-year-round game. Sport's Day was not too far in the future now, and everyone was taking every opportunity to remind me I was a firm favourite for the Junior Victor ludorum. I realised I had an excellent chance to pull it off and was doing a lot of running, both cross-country and sprint training. I determined not to allow the pressure to crush me but to embrace the tag of being the favourite.

We completed some events before the big day, the first being the cross-country race. I had placed second the year before and knew the course very well - a lap of the school field, out of the gates, down to the A50 bypass, along the boring long straight, with heavy traffic roaring next to me and then to the best part of the course, over gates, stiles and farmer's fields looping back into town.

My essential tactic, probably driven by fear of failure, was to get to the front and stay there. So, setting off like a scalded cat at the gun, I checked and saw I was at least thirty yards ahead of the field, running hard, as I turned out of the impressive full-height wrought-iron gates at the entrance to the playing fields. I was then out onto the roads of Uttoxeter's suburbs, winding my way down to the bypass. I did not look back once after coming out of the gates. Forcing a decent pace, with something in hand for the last lap around the track, I was home in seventeen minutes, and six seconds, my best for the course of two and a half miles or so. One down, five more events to go.

The two jump competitions took place one evening after school. I never professed to be a high jumper and just managed third place in that event, a couple of lanky beanpoles edging me out of the top spot. The long jump was a different kettle of fish and an event I liked. I won by a six-inch margin. It was now a matter of the 80 yards, 220 and 440 races held on Sports Day.

The big day came around, and a sizeable crowd of parents, including mine, attended. The cheap black leather spikes I bought at a jumble sale were supposed to help me perform better. I hoped so.

Feeling a little nervous but also quietly confident before the start, I tried to focus. Keeping myself to myself before the races, I warmed up behind the pavilion, where it was quiet, giving myself a pep talk that I just needed to perform to the standards I knew I could.

When the 80 yards came around, I was ready. I saw no one else in my peripheral vision, a 100% flat-out sprint and breasted the tape first. Good. 220 next. The same result, winning by a few yards.

The 440 yards was one of the last events before the relays. Giving it my best shot, to win in style in front of Mum and Dad, was my aim. Running in a middle lane and I could see I was well ahead early on. Coasting the middle section, ensuring that I maintained excellent form and controlled my breathing, I built on my lead. In the final run-in, passing the blur of seated parents, I went into over-drive to win comfortably. Everything had gone to plan, and I was pleased and relieved - the winner of five out of a possible six events.

I met up with Mum and Dad after Sport's Day had finished and after I had competed in a couple of relay events, and they congratulated me warmly. Mum seemed delighted, but I think Dad believed I would win and was not overly effusive. We then had the prize presentations, and some pictures taken by a photographer from the local paper. Keith and Alan were also both prize winners, so our little Cheadle gang had done pretty well.

The term was drawing to a close; we had finished exams, and obviously, sports day was over for another year. The ultimate act of the term was the teachers handing back exam papers and being given both term and exam marks for each subject and our overall ranking in class. It pleased me to come 7th overall, so an improvement on 11th the previous year and a decent school report.

On holiday in Anglesey later on in the summer, Dad dropped the bombshell that the Post Office had offered him a further promotion, which meant that the family would move south to Birmingham later in the year.

Initially, I reflected I would be sad to leave Cheadle and Uttoxeter Grammar. However, I also felt excited about what was to come. A different school. A move close to a city environment. The chance to experience new challenges and opportunities and meet other people. I soon looked forward to the prospect of a new adventure.

I think my brothers both saw things differently. They were a little overwhelmed at moving, being quite happy where they were. Richard was now in the infants at Cheadle County Primary, while Robert was going to be in the top juniors soon.

The plan, Dad said, was for him to start his new job in September as postmaster at Blackheath, a suburb to the west of the city. He would be in lodgings for a while during the working week whilst sorting out a new house, and we would all join up with him in a couple of months if everything worked out as he wanted. I would therefore need to return to Alleyne's for at least a few weeks of the new autumn term.

After absorbing this news, our Anglesey holiday continued much as usual. We checked out the various beaches, according to the prevailing weather. We visited Red Wharf Bay, Rhosneigr, Benlech, Aberffraw and Treaddur but were all unanimous in favouring Newborough.

On one of my regular trips to Mr Jones' farm across the field and over the main road to collect eggs, milk and fresh farm butter, I bumped into Madge, and she excitedly told me the morning's news that Marilyn Monroe had died. They found her dead in bed; she told me. I knew she was a colossal film star, but not much more than that, and rushed back with my provisions to give Mum and Dad the news. It was a big story, and everyone seemed to talk about it for days afterwards.

It was weird being back at school in 3A that September, wearing new long trousers not allowed in the first two years, as I appeared to be a little in limbo. I was just marking time before making a fresh start at Halesowen Grammar school later in the term. I must admit, I did not take schoolwork seriously for a while, convincing myself it was not worth the effort, and messing about in class more than a little.

One time, a teacher, frustrated by my juvenile behaviour, sent me out to stand outside the head's office for the rest of the lesson. Usually, this meant if old Chalky spotted you, he unquestionably whacked you, asking no questions. Outside of his office was a large empty stationery cupboard, so I decided that would be an excellent place to hide until the bell went. The ruse worked, and whilst I heard many comings and goings, I was undisturbed and able to escape a caning, slipping away when the bell went.

Before Dad moved south to take up his new position, there were several presentations and farewells. The Stoke-on-Trent Post Office Sports and Social Club gave Dad a memento of his active time with the group and his efforts serving on various committees and organising several large-scale social events. Hanley Swimming Club also staged a special presentation for him. We had a party at home later with a score or more of our friends and parents. It was both a sad and happy time for us.

Finally, I remember going to chapel just before we were due to leave Cheadle and Grandma was staying with us for a week. The many friends we had made had arranged a gathering. There was a slap-up buffet, speeches, a presentation for us as a family, and a bouquet for Mum. Dad had to make a little speech of thanks, and I remember Grandma saying,

"Look, he's filling up."

Dad tried to keep control of his emotions. I was quite shocked to see tears welling up in his eyes and how emotional he was as he made a heartfelt thank you, and it made me realise that an important and very happy phase of our lives was drawing to a close.

CHAPTER 10

OAK TREE CRESCENT HALESOWEN

Finally, in October, we left the North Staffordshire countryside for a new family life on the periphery of England's second city.

To be fair, I was a little underwhelmed when I first set my eyes on our new home. By my reckoning, Dad was gaining a promotion, which would have meant a larger salary, and thus, we could have afforded a bigger house.

I had failed to understand the intricacies of the housing market and the regional variations in property values. We were moving south, so prices were higher, and therefore budgets were tighter. Our house in Oak Tree Crescent was a typical suburban three-bedroomed semi; it was okay but not a patch on Beech Cottage. It had a telephone, though, a step up from Cheadle, and a number I can still remember to this day, Woodgate 3380. Phone numbers in those days often had letters before the numbers denoting the exchange, so to dial home was WOO 3380. My bedroom, the standard 'box room', was tiny compared to my room in Cheadle, which was a bit of a blow. After some thought, I resigned myself to getting used to it. It was not too bad.

The long narrow back garden was wonderful, though, with plenty of room for football and cricket. Out front, as the road was a quiet cul-de-sac, I had also earmarked it as an additional playground. I quickly developed a game of 'football squash' using the dwarf wall at the edge of the garden. Probably annoying the hell out of the neighbours by constantly kicking a ball noisily against the brickwork, but I was having fun.

I did a little reconnaissance walk around the immediate neighbourhood on our first day, when sent to the local corner shop to get some basic provisions. Going east towards the city, the road next to ours was in Quinton, which was properly in Birmingham, Birmingham 32 as it proudly stated on the street furniture. We were in Halesowen, Worcestershire. I was a little disappointed because I fancied being a sophisticated metropolitan type rather than a parochial country bumpkin. Anyway, that was how I saw it.

Dad then drip-fed me another morsel of news that I guessed he must have been dreading telling me. Halesowen was a rugby-playing school with no football played at all. No school football teams. No house matches. Not even for one term, no football in games lessons. Nothing. Just the aimless egg-chasing game about which I knew not a thing. When he told me this, I could not prevent my face from crumpling as I dissolved into tears whilst trying to be quite brave. No football, this wasn't at all good. Ridiculous.

The other thing he told me was that it was a mixed school. Now, this was something I thought I could live with. I was far more accepting of this piece of news

My uniform was all ready for me: grey trousers, a white shirt, with a smart royal blue blazer. The school motto Ut Filii Lucis Fiatis was under the gold, silver and blue badge on the breast pocket. This translated as 'That we shall become Sons of Light.' I was ready for the off.

I reported to the headteacher, Mr Emmett, as directed and he gave me a bit of a pep talk and an explanation of the class I was to join.

At Uttoxeter, we had the 'A' class and the 'B' class in each year's group. At Halesowen, there were four classes for each year's group, so the institution was twice the size of my previous seat of learning.

Around this time, there was considerable debate in educational circles about the stigma around pupils being labelled 'A', 'B', or 'C' stream. They labelled the forms as 'N', 'S', 'E' and 'W' at my new school, which fooled absolutely nobody.

Physically, as well as in terms of numbers, the school appeared to be twice the size of Uttoxeter. As Mr Emmett gave me a brief tour of the school, I noticed the buildings were newer than at Uttoxeter. They probably dated from the thirties and even later, and were certainly less attractive architecturally than at

Uttoxeter. They lacked the venerable historical stature of Thomas Alleyne's, which I missed.

The North stream was the class who would take their 'O' Levels a year earlier than the rest of their contemporaries. They had thus embarked on their exam subject studies already. They had selected these kids to be fast-tracked because of their performances in their first two years. The school, therefore, allocated me to form 3 South, and they would expect me to select my GCE subjects at the end of the academic year. 3E was the class for those deemed less academically able, while 3W seemed, from what I could make out, to be a bit of an educational dustbin.

The Head knocked on the door of one particular classroom, and all the pupils turned as he presented me to the class as 'the new boy'.

It was a slightly weird experience but reasonably ok as the teacher handed me text and exercise books. The day continued with more of the same, and I wrote the timetable in my rough book as it developed. I was just really thrown in at the deep end, but at least I was a decent swimmer.

A lad called Derek, who became my best friend over the next few weeks, showed me the ropes at break time. I confided in him I was pretty upset that the school did not play football, and he readily sympathised.

"Yeah, a lot of lads feel the same. None of them like rugby, but we all play football at lunchtime on the far quad. I will show you later. We all support the Baggies." (West Bromwich Albion).

Derek's welcoming approach was much appreciated. After lunch, they soon involved me in a mass game with a tennis ball, just like it used to be at Uttoxeter.

Derek appeared to be the best player and was popular with the rest of the boys. However, I could soon display my skills, which had the effect of helping me gain immediate acceptance. My admission to being a Stoke City fan, though, did not meet with any approval. To be fair, Stoke City was doing pretty well in the early part of that season, and I felt they were in with a shout of gaining promotion. I would keep my powder dry, and we would see after the season finished the following spring.

The first week just sailed by, and I found most lessons at a similar level to Uttoxeter. Except for French. At Alleyne's, I had been trying to learn the phonetic way, but this was not the method employed here. I was floundering a little and could never catch up fully. The subject became my only failure at the 'O' levels. However, my vocabulary was quite wide-ranging, and over the years, I have always been able to hold a reasonable conversation in the language. I think my strategy of just mumbling the verb endings in a suitably gallic way did the trick.

The girls, I found, were quite an attractive addition to the classroom. I had never been shy around girls and at Cheadle had a number I knew as friends and those I used to chat with regularly on the school bus. But this was a little different, with half of my classmates being of the fairer sex. I could readily accept this turn of events.

The first games lesson came around, and the gruff PE bloke introduced me to the game of rugby. He was an old Welshman, Dai Davies, who just shuffled around on the touchline in a long shabby overcoat. Shouting out indecipherable instructions and screaming and bawling at some poor unfortunate who had done something wrong in his eyes was his chosen teaching style. I determined to make sure it was not me on the end of his tongue-lashing. I understood the basics about passing backwards and scoring tries, but the scrummage and line-out machinations were beyond me.

It transpired that I could opt to go for a run in games rather than playing rugby. I felt this to be a preferable option to wandering around aimlessly on a muddy field with some scruffy old Welshman yelling from the touchline.

This state of affairs, on reflection, was quite ironic given that the game of rugby became so important to me in later years. I later played first-team level for several decent clubs and enjoyed a thirty-year playing career. Being keen, fit, reasonably fast, and with good hand-eye coordination, I took to the game readily in my early twenties. If Taff had offered guidance and encouragement when I first went to Halesowen, things might have worked out differently. But it would never be forthcoming with the old Welshman at the helm.

On one occasion early on at Halesowen, I did not endear myself to him much. He called out for me and another lad to fetch a large package for him. We would find it in somewhere called the foyer. We both ran off in the general direction of the main school buildings he had shown with his hand. Both assumed that the other knew where or what a 'fireyeah' was. Unfortunately, neither of us did and had to go back and seek further clarification meekly. So, he had probably concluded I was thick as well as being a rugby denier.

During the early weeks at our new Birmingham home, out exploring our surroundings as a family, we drove down Manor Lane, close to our house. We drove past a sign stating 'Manor Abbey, Home of Halesowen Athletic and Cycling Club'.

"Dad, can we go in and have a look, please?"

He indulged me, and we motored down the approach road where there were club buildings and a large banked concrete cycle velodrome with an athletic track in the middle.

"Wow, a proper athletics club can I join, please, Dad?"

"We'll see", was the non-committal reply.

I was persistent, though, and after a bit of pestering, he took me down to the club, and I signed up as a junior member. From then on, I regularly trained with other club members, going on road runs on Tuesday and Thursday evenings and taking part in cross-country races on Saturdays.

Dad had found a swimming and water polo club about ten miles away at Stourbridge and was already enjoying playing for them. I think he discovered the place when in lodgings before we moved down to the area as a family. He was keen to find somewhere to carry on playing his favourite sport. I used to go along occasionally when he had games and try to get in the water for a throwabout before the match started. So, I was still keen to continue with my water polo.

There was also a regular Sunday morning training session at Stourbridge, and I looked forward to going along with Dad. I would do a few lengths of swimming, working on my speed, fitness and techniques at all the strokes and then we would have a practice polo match.

That autumn in 1962, even without my heightened awareness of current affairs, I would not have failed to understand that something very frightening and even unprecedented was happening on the world stage. Potentially catastrophic events were in prospect as the world's two superpowers, the USA and

USSR, played out a high-stakes standoff, and threatening world peace.

I remember Dad speaking with some of his friends at Stourbridge in serious and hushed tones. I picked up keywords like 'crisis' and 'nuclear warheads' and talk of 'blowing us all to smithereens.'

For a month from mid-October, the world held its breath as a game of cat and mouse, threat and counter-threat, unfolded. The Russians planned the installation of missiles with nuclear capability on the island of Cuba at the invitation of President Fidel Castro. Ominously just ninety miles from American soil, this was obviously unacceptable to the American administration.

The two leading proponents, Presidents Khrushchev and Kennedy, played out their hands. To the immense relief in the west, Khrushchev finally blinked first, and the Russians withdrew the missiles. The world had averted a nuclear catastrophe by the narrowest of margins.

As it became known, the Cuban Missile Crisis led to the installation of the hotline between Washington and Moscow. This allowed speedy direct telephone communication between the two world leaders to avoid such cliff-edge dramas occurring again. Whilst relationships remained difficult, the Cuban affair was the low point of the Cold War. This period lasted from the end of World War 2 until the dissolution of the USSR in 1991. A long time.

This autumn was also a sad time for me as Grandad passed away because of a heart condition at 75. He had visited us a few weeks earlier and seemed fit and well, helping Dad construct a lean-to extension for additional storage at the side of the house. So it was a bit of a shock to hear the news. I remember Dad and me having a tearful conversation about what a lovely human being he had been and what an influence he had on both our lives.

"So sad. Dad was a wonderful man and a good father, and I owed him such a lot," was Dad's conclusion.

Grandad certainly lived longer than my maternal grandfather, who I only vaguely remembered, as he died in his early sixties when I was a toddler. Both of their womenfolk, though, were to live until their nineties.

With the world back on a relatively even keel politically, I just knuckled down to getting myself up to speed with my various subjects at school. It was probably as well I had a year before deciding, apart from the core subjects of English, Maths and French, what other topics I would opt for at 'O' level.

I seemed to have a fair amount of homework daily and would retire to my room after tea for a good couple of hours to tackle it. My room was freezing, as the central heating radiators did not extend to the upstairs of the house. Mum had bought a slim, simple, convection heater to improve my situation. I often resorted to perching on top of it while working at getting some warmth into my body.

The homework thing, though, was a good reason (or excuse) not to get involved with the redecorating programme. My parents embarked on a full house redecoration programme with their customary missionary zeal. My middle brother was now a designated decorating apprentice and seemed to relish the job. This pleased me.

I was happy completing most of my homework without help, but I appeared to be a long way behind in Latin. I would not be studying this moribund language beyond the following year, so I coasted along. One girl I got on well with was a bit of a Latin genius, so when homework for the subject was due, I used to meet her in the cloakroom before school. I would copy out her efforts, being clever enough to put in some odd errors to avoid suspicion.

While still going to Stourbridge every Sunday to do some swimming training and practice water polo with Dad, I now thought of myself as more of an athlete than a swimmer. I enjoyed going to Halesowen A &CC for the club nights and taking part in cross-country and road races on the weekends. I think Dad was okay about this, although I knew he would appreciate me continuing to improve my aquatic skills, and particularly becoming a decent polo player.

That winter of 1963 was extremely harsh and became known as the 'Big Freeze'. Snow fell in mid-December and lasted through to early March in many parts of the country.

I remember taking part in one cross-country race and doing well when the snowy weather started and before the ground froze totally underneath the surface of snow and ice. Being small and light relative to the men, I ran over the top of the ploughed fields on the route. They all struggled, sinking through the snow into the mud below with every step. The experience of coming home in front of many older runners was enjoyable, but I knew I was running with a considerable advantage.

I also won the Boxing Day Handicap race that year, primarily because of my generous time advantage. The air was so cold that I could feel it burning into my lungs. My legs were mottled red. I was certainly glad to have a reviving hot shower at the end and get back home for a family celebration meal. Proudly taking my prize of a trophy and an impressive pigskin wallet with me.

The extraordinarily long period of snowy conditions meant we went sledging regularly that winter with my brothers and a few new local mates. We lived at the top of Mucklow Hill, part of the escarpment which ran down to Halesowen town. So there were plenty of potential tracks just a few minutes from home in the sizeable area of undeveloped land known as the Leasowes.

There was a report in the local paper that January that a brand new swimming pool was being built in Halesowen. Before long, Dad had become heavily involved in the formation of the new swimming club, which would become based at the facility. They appointed him the inaugural Hon. Sec. of Halesowen Swimming Club after he turned up to a public meeting about the formation of such an entity that was announced in the local paper. Endless committee meetings took up lots of his time, but he seemed to thrive on getting involved with the project.

The inauguration of the club took place in May 1963, and being fickle and impressed by the incredible new facility, I switched sporting allegiances. I reverted to being primarily a swimmer. Club nights on a Friday took up the whole evening from 6 pm through to 10 pm. The club catered for swimming lessons in the early part of the evening, training sessions and technique improvement for various ages and levels came after that. Family 'Splash Time' followed, and the evening ended with water polo practice. The pool became a home from home every Friday night for all the family.

A month before the Halesowen Swimming Club swung into action for the first time, Stoke City held off the challenge of

Chelsea to win the Second Division championship. The Potters had gained a promotion to the top table of the English game. They secured the title with a two-nil home win over Luton Town, Matthews dribbling around the goalie in his inimitable style to net the second and clinch the win. Incredibly, this was *thirty years* after he had first helped Stoke to achieve success in winning the Second Division title. Bragging rights were now mine at school as the Baggies finished only a modest 14th position in the First Division that season.

School exams came around in June, and I did ok. I think I got two or three first places, and I placed in the top four or five in other subjects. The school did not publish a class league table, but my performances quite satisfied me. I felt quite ready for the next stage, which was the two years of working towards 'O' levels.

Career-wise at this stage, I was thinking of nothing more than going to Loughborough Colleges and studying PE for three years. While they had designed the Loughborough course to train teachers, I was confident I did not want a lengthy teaching career. I felt I was more entrepreneurial and would like to be in business on my own account someday. I just needed to work out exactly how this might come about, but whatever I did would definitely be involved with the world of sports and leisure. Three years at the top PE college would be a good start, and undoubtedly enjoyable.

My parents felt that my intention to go to a teacher training institution was an honourable choice. They believed it would lead me to a worthy if unexciting forty-odd years in the blackboard jungle. Dad had obviously committed to his Post Office career from an early age, and he presumed I would follow a similar route in the educational world. I was happy to let them think that.

Dad must have decided the trek north-westwards up to Anglesey was too far away to drive now we lived further to the south; so we sought other holiday destinations more directly westwards, in mid-Wales. We then seemed to settle on New Quay in Cardiganshire. The exact location was a farmer's field at Cai Bach, a couple of miles away from the pretty little harbour town. We went away there for Whit Week and then returned for our main two-week break at the end of July.

There were no facilities other than a cold water tap and an outside loo in the farmyard a couple of hundred metres away. As we had done in Anglesey, this was basic camping with cooking over a campfire inside a stone hearth that Dad constructed. He had negotiated with the farmer to use the field for a modest rate, and we could fetch milk, eggs and butter regularly from the farmhouse. We had the site to ourselves, and for us boys, it was a wonderful playground.

Over the stone wall marking the edge of the farmer's land was a steep wooded slope. At the bottom, a small stream meandered a few hundred yards to where it disgorged into the sea. This was the regular route we took to the beach, down the pretty path at the side of the stream, festooned with flowers. We would also breathe in the distinctive aroma of wild garlic as we walked. The path followed the river to what we designated 'our beach'. This is where we made our base for the day.

With its attractive harbour, complete with colourful fishing boats bobbing about, New Quay was around an arc of sandy beach a mile or so away to the south. We would set up camp on Cai Bach beach and have the place very much to ourselves.

As we were now a little older, Mum and Dad were happy to let us paddle across to New Quay in the old dependable inflatable canoe. We would perch Richard on the bow, giving him a free ride.

We would be in their sightline all the way over, so they deemed it safe enough for us to undertake the journey without direct adult supervision.

Sometimes Mum and Dad would take the canoe over themselves and we would just stay and play on the beach.

The holidays were quite idyllic, but straightforward. As long as it was not pouring down with rain, we would be at the beach, swimming, canoeing, building dams on the stream, exploring rock pools, and catching crabs. If the weather was not so agreeable, we would probably just mooch around New Quay, dodging showers and eating ice creams.

Further along from where our stream met the ocean, there was an area of beach used by people staying at the caravan park sited above. We would sometimes go along there and start up a cricket game. Like a benign Pied Piper, Dad would soon have encouraged loads of additional participants, children and adults to join in. We would play for ages before collectively deciding we had enjoyed enough cricket for a while and all sprint into the sea for a refreshing swim.

Simple picnic food prepared by Mum at lunchtime would sustain us. The evening meal would comprise the usual meat and two veg combinations out of tins, heated by the campfire, with homemade cakes and pies for dessert. The same pattern we had become used to in Anglesey.

We would not leave the beach until eight if the weather was perfect, so there was not much of the evening left after eating and washing up. If we went up to the tent earlier, we might go out for a walk around the local lanes after supper. Occasionally, we might drive up to New Quay for a walk around the harbour and look at the boats.

While we were on holiday, news broke of an audacious robbery that captured the entire country's imagination. A gang who tampered with a trackside signal caused a train to make an unscheduled stop. This was no ordinary train, though. It was the overnight mail train, stashed full of cash. The train robbers then forcibly entered the special travelling post office coaches, ransacking the colossal amount of £2.6m (a 2022 equivalent of £55 million).

There was a certain amount of public sympathy and respect for the sheer ingenuity of the heist. However, the villains were careless with the number of clues they left at the remote farmhouse where they holed up. After following up on these leads and additional long hours of painstaking police work, the authorities brought most of the gang to justice early into the new year.

However, the public perception of the thirty-year sentences handed down to the ringleaders was one of shock. The establishment was undoubtedly sending out an obvious message. I suppose my thinking about the heist was that it was an audacious robbery, and the sentences were out of all proportion. The jail terms handed down were about the amount they stole, which I felt was not relevant. Robbery was robbery. The problem was that someone viciously assaulted the driver with an iron bar

during the raid and that coloured the prosecution's view and
helped determine the sentences.

114

CHAPTER 11

A FOURTH FORMER

Back at school in September, for me, meant a move up to 4S. Our form mistress was the strict Maths teacher, the always severely dressed, hair in a bun, Mrs Waller, of whom many classmates were wary. She had a fierce tongue, did not suffer fools gladly, and many of my fellow pupils regarded her as some sort of harridan. As I was doing well at maths, I got on well with her, although you would never dream of taking any liberties.

The classroom itself was a significant improvement from our previous years. It was a large and high-ceilinged ground floor room with full-height French doors leading out to a small grassed area bounded by a low brick wall. We in 4S regarded this as ours and ours alone and it became a base at breaks and lunchtimes.

By now, we had chosen our particular options to study alongside the core subjects. These were English Language, English Literature, Maths and a language, in my case French, in preference to Latin. I had decided on Geography, History and two General Science options known as GS1 and GS2. I wanted to continue with biology, but this apparently was not possible because of how the school had organised the options.

This September also meant a school change for my eleven-year-old brother, Robert, moving from Lapal Lane primary to the Hill and Cakemore Secondary Modern. The school was conveniently located just down Long Lane, only about half a mile from our house. From what I could understand, it was not a happy move, and he did not settle well there. Also, Richard, the youngest sibling, did not take kindly to having to continue at primary school without his big brother, so there was further discontent.

While both my brothers were unhappy with school life, I believed they were also a little resentful about the general disruption to their day-to-day lives caused by having to leave Cheadle; I felt there was little I could do.

On the sporting front, I persuaded Dad to write to the school, to Taff specifically, to ask if he could release me from games lessons to go to Halesowen's pool to undertake additional training. I was progressing well with my swimming. Taff, surprisingly to me, agreed to this request. In reality, though, I thought it did not bother him where I went.

I devised a training schedule along with my club coach, Frank, and put in the mileages necessary to improve my times. That is very much the nature of swimming. Endless lengths ploughing up and down in the heavily chlorinated water or else, when doing the backstroke, which was then my best event, looking up forever at the ceiling. The reward, though, was feeling more powerful in the water and gaining a more muscular physique. I wanted to grow taller and heavier, but that natural process was taking its time. I was not an early developer and was thus at a sizeable disadvantage to lads who found themselves to be six foot plus and over twelve stones at a young age.

Besides the club nights and swimming on my own in games lessons, I went to local Midlands Amateur Swimming Association junior training initiatives organised and run by top ASA coaches or National Technical Officers (NTOs). My favourite coach was an avuncular Scot, Bert Kinnear, who I got on very well with. Attending sessions meant getting buses or grabbing lifts with coaches and other swimmers to travel to pools all over the Black Country. Sessions would be for an hour and a half or more of heavy training on a couple of other nights in the week. I had by now stopped going to Halesowen A and CC, and my career as an athlete was in abeyance.

On Saturday mornings, I took a couple of bus rides to Bearwood, along Hagley Road towards the city. I then travelled to Smethwick by another bus to train for two hours at the old Victorian swimming pool at Rolfe Street Baths.

I enjoyed the sessions there as it was a short pool, only twenty yards long, and the mixed squad used to focus on sprint training. We would also do a lot of fun, but competitive relays and flailing limbs would churn the waters up into a boiling cauldron. It was an excellent social mix as well, with everyone working hard but having a good laugh, with a bit of room for some flirtatious liaisons sometimes before heading home.

I always remember going home on the bus with a feeling of euphoria afterwards. I would have pleasantly aching muscles from the hard physical workout and be buzzing from the complete experience.

That summer, a major news scandal dominated the airwaves for several weeks, culminating in the trial of the society osteopath, Stephen Ward. This became known as the Profumo affair. Profumo was a Tory minister in Macmillan's government who appeared to share a certain Christine Keeler's charms with a Russian naval attaché, becoming a potential security risk. Ward affected the introductions.

Profumo lied to parliament about the affair, bringing about the end of his political career. And, in due course, the downfall of Macmillan and the Conservatives, letting in Harold Wilson and the Labour party at the 1964 General Election. Ward, believing the establishment had made him a scapegoat, took a fatal drug overdose before they concluded the trial.

A lad at school I knocked around with shared the same name as the osteopath. Our head, obviously not wishing his school to be associated with such a scandal, enquired if he would be happy to be referred to by his second name, James, and drop the 'Stephen' appellation. It amazed Stephen that the headteacher made such a suggestion, as it did me when I heard about it. He declined to change his name and thought the very proposition to be absurd. I totally agreed.

1963 to me also seemed to be when British music came out of the shadows of the American scene. Until this point, artists from across the Atlantic dominated popular music. Some might have considered British music to have come to the fore a little earlier. But at fourteen, my awareness of the surge in the popularity of British music was very much about this time. In spare moments between lessons or breaks, our little gang would discuss the merits of the latest pop releases. This activity probably took over from kicking a football around, which we had now left for the younger boys.

As well as discussing the merits of the Beatles, the Rolling Stones and the Animals, there was also considerable interest in the young American folk-rock singer Bob Dylan. He had released an album called 'Freewheelin' Bob Dylan'. Its iconic cover showed Dylan with his collar up, hunched against the cold, walking with his then girlfriend. It featured such classics as 'Blowin' in the wind' and 'Don't think twice it's alright', which made a big impression on us all.

Other Brits who emerged this year include the Dave Clark Five, The Tremeloes, The Searchers, Gerry and the Pacemakers, Billy J Kramer and Freddie and the Dreamers, amongst many others.

I had got hold of a secondhand Dansette record player with the renowned Garrard SP25 deck, which was obligatory amongst the cognoscenti. I did not bother about singles, but I built a modest collection of LPs. This collection started with the Beatles' first album, released earlier in the year, 'Please Please Me.' I kept these precious possessions tucked away in my bedroom, away from potentially inquisitive siblings.

My second LP purchase was the Beatles' second offering, 'With the Beatles,' which knocked its predecessor off the top rung. It had been there for the best part of the year. The Beatles were undoubtedly making a massive impact on the world of popular music in 1963.

We did not get official pocket money, although Mum and Dad were quite generous about giving us money for whatever was needed, within reason. They gave me daily bus fare money, but I would normally walk to save the two-pence ha'penny fare each way. (By scrimping, I saved up over time the 4 pounds and 10 shillings required to make my record player purchase.) Continuing to take the walking option allowed me to save sufficient funds to buy the albums to play on my precious new acquisition.

My friend Derek was into his music as well, and at one time, there was talk of us, with a couple of others forming a band. With all my training commitments, I decided I could not commit to learning an instrument, but I would be happy to sing and play the harmonica! We talked about it a lot, but we got very little further than that. But I remember Derek buying a cheap electric keyboard from Woolworth's, which actually sounded somewhat like the classic Hammond organ, and he learned a few tunes on that.

***

If I were a bit late for school or had too much stuff to carry, I would take the bus, just walking down our crescent and up the next road, through a gulley to come out at the Stag and Three Horseshoes pub. This was on the main Hagley Road and close to the bus stop. I would sometimes go over the zebra crossing to the newsagents to get some sweets or chocolate if I had time.

The old boy who ran the place was a bit of an anachronism. He had a persistent, wheezy cough and was constantly hacking up something disgusting from the bottom of his lungs. He would then form this into a decent missile shape with his tongue and send the resultant globule into a stainless steel spittoon located some feet away on the floor. It would land with a satisfying and resounding ping. I think the polite term for this action is expectorating, but my mates and I, who quite enjoyed the little cabaret act, called it gobbing.

***

One evening that Autumn, something happened that affected the entire world. Everyone around at the time could recall decades later precisely where they were when they heard the devastating news. For our family, this was easy. It was a Friday night, so we were all at the Halesowen pool.

On the 22nd of November 1963, in those pre-mobile phone days, the news spread rapidly from person to person along the poolside. Kennedy was dead. Someone called Lee Harvey Oswald assassinated the handsome and charismatic young American President, John F Kennedy. The whole place was in shock, but it was true. The leader of the free world was dead.

I was stunned by the news. The reaction of many of the adults around also shocked me. Many women were in tears and the men, visibly shaken, spoke with friends in hushed whispers about what this seismic event would mean to world order and stability. They were probably thinking back a few short months to when the world had held its collective breath as the Cuban Missile Crisis unfolded. That episode had brought about the genuine threat of a nuclear war between the two world superpowers. That Friday

119

night, the world seemed to me to be a very fragile place, and I remember feeling quite desolate and fearful about the future.

Inevitably, the situation settled down, and President Lyndon Johnson took over the reins in the United States. In the early days, I watched a few current affairs programmes until I felt reassured that the world, for all its troubles, was not teetering on the brink.

One frequently aired topic was that the Americans were becoming more heavily involved in Vietnam. The USA had a vast and growing military presence in the south of this long slender country in Indo-China, formerly a French colony. The build-up of troops was to provide support, ostensibly, for the South Vietnamese in their war against the communist Viet Cong of the country's north. As Britain did not have any direct involvement, news coverage was not overly extensive. Although I remember we were all aware of the conflict at school, and that awareness grew over the next few years.

That December, Halesowen Swimming Club held their inaugural annual gala, where I picked up a few trophies. Dad also arranged a water polo match as a finale to the event between the County Champions, Stourbridge, and the rest of the county. I had some game time in the match, which pleased me immensely. I was coming along ok as a player.

There was a swimming club Christmas party soon afterwards. I was getting on nicely with a charming young girl, dancing to the Beatles' latest release, 'I wanna hold your hand', which was topping the charts. Dad came up to speak to me, to ask about what events I wanted to swim in an upcoming gala.

"Not now, Dad. I'll speak to you later," I stage-whispered and glared, and he took the hint.

Christmas 1963 was the usual round of family celebrations, this year enhanced by several social events and parties at the swimming club or with friends from the organisation. We did not visit Boston.

Back at school for the new term, with my training commitments and homework, I found I did not watch that much television. I might watch the odd Steptoe and Son instalment and any sport. Mainly, however, I was happy to go to bed early, read and listen to Radio Luxembourg on my upgraded transistor radio, a recent Christmas present.

My reading material, selected from the local library, mainly around this time comprised sporting biographies such as 10km runner Gordon Pirie's *Running Wild,* the great Australian middle distance exponent Herb Elliott's *The Golden Mile,* and Murray Halberg's and Dorothy Hyman's autobiographies. I also read the literary efforts by British swimmers Anita Lonsbrough, Ian Black and Judy Grinham, as well as Aussies Jon and Ilsa Konrads, the great Dawn Fraser and Murray Rose, amongst others.

The Australian swimmers' tales were all about training in the sunshine in large outdoor pools. It was a far cry from my reality of cold and foggy mornings or evenings at old Victorian baths somewhere in the Black Country.

I also distinctly remember reading of the brilliant middle-distance runner Herb Elliott training in the sunshine at Portsea, Victoria, under his coach, the formidable Percy Cerutty. The latter was a brilliant advocate of gaining endurance by running up and down dunes and through the waves on the foreshore. I remember trying to emulate this when on holiday.

The other biography of a great miler I read was Roger Bannister's *First Four Minutes.* I committed this sentence to memory,

The first time the mile was run in under four minutes was by Bannister, a medical student, with a time of three minutes fifty-nine point four seconds at Iffley Road, Oxford, on the 6th of May 1954.

I was to meet the great man some years later when I was a humble assistant leisure centre manager. He visited us in his role as chairperson of the Sports Council.

That January saw the start of a television programme, my brothers and I, along with countless millions of other youngsters the length and breadth of the country, rapidly became avid fans of. Top of the Pops became required weekly viewing, initially on a Wednesday and then changing to a regular Thursday night slot. This led to performances, songs, and personalities being dissected and debated ad infinitum in school on Fridays. The first show featured Dusty Springfield, the Rolling Stones, The Dave Clark Five, the Hollies, and the Swinging Blue Jeans. The Beatles closed the show with their number one, "I wanna hold your hand". What a line-up!

Dad occasionally caught a glimpse,

"They all need a good haircut" was his comment, particularly about the Stones.

When he saw the exceptionally hirsute American band, The Pretty Things, later in the year, he was beyond words other than a spluttered

"Whaaaat!"

I remember the raucous drum-led Dave Clark Five tunes 'Glad all Over' and later, 'Bits and Pieces' had us raiding the kitchen cupboards for pots and pans and other potential percussion instruments. We would play along and make a right old racket. Mum and Dad, at these times, sensibly retreated to the relative tranquillity of the front room.

The swinging sixties had now well and truly landed, and teenagers were a new tribe who had found their voice. Grown-ups would have to take notice!

As well as Top of the Pops, I also liked to watch whatever sport was on television, if schoolwork commitments allowed.

In January I remember catching something of a sporting rarity with the British duo of Nash and Dixon winning the two-man bobsleigh event at the Winter Olympics at Innsbruck.

Whilst not a massive fan of boxing, early into the new year, it intrigued me how the brash young Cassius Clay, a winner at Light Heavyweight level at the tender age of 18 at the Rome Olympics in 1960, would perform in his next fight. This contest pitched him against the brooding, heavy punching and intimidating Sonny Liston, the current heavyweight World Champion. Soon to change his name to Mohammed Ali after converting to Islam, Clay entered the ring, demonstrating his fancy footwork as an eight-to-one underdog. He shocked the watching millions by pulling off a fantastic victory. It was unmissable stuff.

Around this time, I struggled to read the blackboard from where I usually sat towards the back of any classroom. I had to resolve matters by sitting closer to the front, but even that did not help. There was obviously an issue with my vision. I was short-sighted and explained to Dad that I could not see clearly at a distance. He did not seem to understand this, as his vision was still almost perfect. But he said he would arrange for me to go to an optician in Blackheath for a check-up and an eye test.

We went along one afternoon; him having to leave the office for a short time. After undergoing all the various tests, the specialist sat us down and explained the situation. I was short-sighted and would need to wear glasses.

"Will the situation improve, and he might not need them long term?" Dad enquired hopefully.

"No. John has myopia, and his sight will get worse. He will need them for the rest of his life," was the curt and unambiguous response.

This brutal and tactless pronouncement caused the tears to prick in my eyes, although I tried to blink them back. It did not seem fair. A 'four eyes' forever. It certainly would not help my sport or, I believed, my opportunities with the fairer sex.

Shit, what a bummer. I thought. They then hauled me off to have a look at the 'milky bar kid' range of display options, as this was well before the designer frame market took off. The free national health service frames were not anything that would enhance anyone's appearance, let alone those of a dashing young athlete in his prime.

I eventually chose the least worst option and decided to just wear them to see the blackboard as and when I needed to. So, that happened for the next couple of years; I carried the offending articles around in their case and just whipped them out to decipher some illegible chalky scrawl as required.

The optician with the less-than-perfect bedside manner was right, though. My eyesight did not improve; in fact, it became worse, and I inevitably wore them constantly. His diagnosis was that a bout of German measles I had as a toddler caused my myopia.

I eventually persuaded Dad to fork out for some more acceptable frames rather than being stuck with the particularly naff NHS choices. In the end, I just had to accept the fact. I wore glasses.

Derek and our gang continued to chat at school regularly and enthusiastically about the current pop music scene. I remember going to school one day when the Searcher's single 'Needles and

Pins' had just come onto the market. We were all taken with how the group sang "needles and pinza" in the refrain.

Although there were plenty of chats about favourite bands and songs, the prospect of us forming a group would never get out of the starting blocks. Derek had turned instead to comedy, and he and I used to get together, and I would help him write short comedy sketches just for a bit of fun.

I didn't realise until later that he was submitting these efforts to the renowned BBC radio producer Humphrey Barclay. The latter was in charge of a new anarchic programme called *I'm sorry I'll read that again*. This was a top-rated cult comedy programme and a precursor to a lot of hilarious and rebellious humour, from the Goodies to the Monty Python team, amongst others.

Funnily enough, Bill Oddie, who was a major contributor to the programme and later became a Goodie, attended our school a few years earlier. He later moved to a direct grant grammar school in Birmingham. He even used to live down Oak Tree Crescent, so he was a close neighbour at one stage.

Derek had several sketches accepted for the show. We enjoyed listening to the programme and hearing his name check in the final credits. Contributors also included such future notables as Cleese, Chapman and Idle.

***

We were all still going regularly to the Long Lane Methodist Chapel down the road. I was also doing bible study classes one night a week to prepare for some scripture examinations Dad wanted me to take. I still have two Honours certificates from those days.

However, I was questioning several aspects of religion though and would like to have stopped attending Sunday school. I was reluctant, though, to broach the issue with my parents, not wishing to rock the boat.

That summer, though, I benefited from my chapel affiliations by going camping for a few days in Wales, somewhere around Tenby, with a group of fellow teenagers. Some young church leaders, in their early twenties, led the trip. I think we had a decent enough time with lots of rock climbing and swimming in the sea, but what I remember most about the holiday was driving home in our hired minibus overnight. We reached Clent Hills, a local landmark near Halesowen, in time to walk up to the summit and watch the dawn break over the Birmingham cityscape to the east. It was quite magical. And quite a novelty for me to see the dawn break,

I also remember that summer, a young lad around my age attended chapel from an Indian background. We used to pal around a bit, and I was walking along with him one day when a group of youths, a couple of years older than us, approached us menacingly.

"What are you doing with the Paki? Are you a fucking Paki lover?"

"He is Indian, and he is my mate", I responded firmly, or at least as firmly as I could, trying to disguise the uneasy fear I felt.

I thought they would beat us up, but by holding our ground, they just walked on, throwing abuse over their shoulders as they sauntered off.

I just could not understand their mindset at all.

***

My swimming was going well, and I had some success locally in competitions against other clubs and the County Championships. I also seemed to have gained an unwanted fan club. A couple of girls a year or two below me were swimming club members and led the support for our team, and me in particular. They would sit on the poolside surrounded by 'gonks' which were the popular thing of the moment. They used these furry little round gnomic creatures with enormous eyes as mascots and had them decked out in the club colours of blue and gold.

Unfortunately, these girls took the support to the extreme at school. I was less than amused to see that in many classrooms throughout the school, someone had carved large letters to proclaim 'I love Stan' and 'Stan is fab' and similar into desk lids. There was quite an epidemic of such graffiti.

It horrified me to be summoned to see the headteacher one day to explain the origins of this vandalism. Initially, it seemed he wanted to be reassured that I had not carried out the inscriptions myself. It amazed me he thought I could be some sort of narcissist and strongly refuted any such thing. I explained it

125

might be somebody from the swimming club, and he stopped any further inquisition. Presumably, he made enquiries elsewhere, but I was off the hook. Highly embarrassing, though.

Dai Davies, the PE and Games master I barely had anything to do with day to day, approached me one day and showed me a letter he had received about the English Schools Swimming Championships. They held this event annually. It would appear that they divided the country into distinct divisions, which selected teams of swimmers to compete in the annual championships every autumn. Halesowen GS was in Division 6 of the English schools' districts, which comprised Shropshire, Herefordshire and Worcestershire, a large but essentially rural catchment area. The letter was an invitation to put pupils forward to compete in the Division 6 trials. These were to be held in a month.

"Are you interested?" he inquired.

"Yes. I have never heard of it, but yes, I would like to go."

With that, he just left me the letter and walked off.

I competed at the RAF pool in Cosford outside Wolverhampton and became the Division 6 Boy's 110-yard backstroke champion a few weeks later. The Championships were to be held in Grimsby later in the year, and I was going to represent the three counties.

***

That summer, we went to the beautiful area around St David's in Pembrokeshire for our major summer holiday for a change, camping in a proper site with a shower block and a shop. We used the wonderful Whitesands Bay as our beachside base. There were also other superb beaches in the area we visited, such as Broadhaven and Druidston. I felt that the Pembrokeshire beaches were amongst the best I had ever seen.

The Whitesands beach was only a short walk from the campsite. I remember being friendly with a couple of girls my age on the beach, and I invited them back to the tent. Mum and Dad gave approval, and we listened to the Top 40 being broadcast by Radio Caroline.

Caroline was one of the new and deliciously illegal pirate radio stations which had started broadcasting that year. The idea of youthful new DJs playing all the splendid music around rather than listening to boring, staid old BBC presenters seemed to me to represent a sea change in the grand scheme of things.

We spent several hours listening to the latest bestselling songs, relaxing on sun loungers around Mum and Dad's transistor. I was in seventh heaven, sharing my sunny afternoon with a couple of pretty girls. I loved the music, appreciating the superb bluesy voice of Eric Burdon on the Animals' 'House of the Rising Sun' as well as Jagger on 'It's All Over.' We enjoyed songs by the Hollies, The Beach Boys and a new girl singer, not much older than us, Lulu. Manfred Mann topped the charts with 'Do Wah Diddy'. I also loved lead vocalist Paul Jones' smoky voice. I still do all these years on.

CHAPTER 12

O LEVEL YEAR

As we became fifth formers, our base moved next door to our previous classroom and still had the advantage of our private bit of space outside the tall French doors. We would sit on the wall before registration or at lunchtime and chat about sport and music in fine weather.

The Baggies supporters would be full of comments about their team, and I succumbed to persuasion and go along to the Hawthorns a couple of times and see Jeff Astle, Clive Clark, and Tony Brown in action. However, my swimming commitments prevented me from going regularly. Or gave me an excuse.

Also, in the fifth form, thinking it might be a useful string to my bow, for being accepted at Loughborough, I started playing hockey. I quickly reached a level where I could command a place in the first eleven. I reflected it was weird that while the school played rugby and hockey, football was a no-no. Anyway, I became a reasonable exponent at hockey, playing in the forward line and scoring a few goals. However, playing on a bumpy, muddy grass pitch was not conducive to skilful, fast hockey. It was now on my c.v., though, and might help with my application.

October 1964 saw the start of the Tokyo Olympics. I raced down early every morning to hear the latest news on the BBC radio, the update programme being introduced by the catchy theme tune 'Tokyo Melody', which became a big hit that year. These were the first Olympics to be broadcast live thanks to new satellite technology so the Tokyo games resonated strongly with me as I could also catch some of the action on television.

I followed the Games avidly over the two weeks and felt at a bit of a loss when it was all over.

I followed Scottish sprint swimmer Bobby McGregor's progress, who I believed had a splendid chance at the 100m freestyle event. In the end, he was just edged out by the American swimming great, Don Schollander, but came home with a creditable silver.

In athletics, I felt the British team captain Robbie Brightwell would get into the medals in the 400m, but unfortunately, he came in a disappointing 4th. His fiancée, Ann Packer, had also failed to live up to expectations with her silver in the 400m where she had started as a firm favourite. Also down to run the 800m, a distance at which she had little experience, she had decided not to run in favour of going shopping in downtown Tokyo. Brightwell's relative failure in his event brought about a change of heart and she competed.

She ended up storming to victory in the longer race, with the television cameras capturing the joyful embrace at the finish between her and Brightwell. Brightwell was also to pick up silver in the 4 x 400m relay event, so he at least had something to show for his efforts, and his wife-to-be was not the only one in the household who was to experience the view from the podium. Three short years later, he was to become one of my lecturers at Loughborough.

I enjoyed watching other great British medal-winning performances, including those achieved by Mary Rand, who captured gold, silver and bronze, and was an outstanding all-around athlete. Also, successful in Tokyo was the tremendous Welsh long jumper, Lyn 'the leap' Davies, who struck gold in his speciality. Years later, when I was managing sports centres, and he was an ambassador for Welsh gym and sports hall equipment manufacturer Powersports, we had a drunken late night standing long jump competition. I don't recall the outcome.

We also had a General Election in the middle of the Olympics, although this significant political event did not particularly capture my imagination. According to the press, the electorate ousted the conservatives because of the Profumo scandal – and Harold Wilson and the Labour Party took over the helm.

The excitement of the Olympics (and I suppose the Election) over it was back to focusing on the humdrum world of school routine and swimming training. As well as pool sessions, I was also now doing some weight training at my coach, Frank's house, where he had set up a rudimentary gym in his garage for a few of us to use. We had other land-based training sessions programmed into the week, with one held in a school gym before a pool session. This Tuesday night programme was the hardest of the week, involving a very strenuous circuit training stint followed by an intensive hour in the new Coseley pool with Bert Kinnear in charge.

Dependent on age, sex, strength and fitness, they designed the circuit sessions to be up to three circuits of about a dozen exercises. We performed three green, orange or red graded circuits or combinations thereof, with the red programme demanding the most repetitions.

After training for a few weeks, a couple of other lads and I raised the bar somewhat. We caused the introduction of a new purple category. We were flying up and down ropes and wall bars, leaping vaulting boxes and performing endless pull-ups and press-ups for three purple lung-bursting circuits.

One evening after the circuit session, Bert told us on poolside that he had read of a young Australian lad who had swum a mile butterfly the previous week. He said that if anyone wanted to try this gruelling challenge instead of swimming the standard programme, we were welcome to do so. Of course, my brothers-in-arms from the gym and I picked up the gauntlet and prepared to tackle this event. We all managed it, but it would not be something we would want to repeat. It was exhausting, but I enjoyed the achievement.

Getting to Grimsby later that year, I realised something that at some level I had known for a while. I used to subscribe to the Swimming Times (having formerly been an avid reader of Athletics Weekly). From times recorded by the top performers, I could see that whilst I was a decent enough swimmer, I was way off being anyone who would make it to the top table. At Grimsby, I rubbed shoulders with International swimmers, but I was just an also-ran from little old Halesowen and did not even make the finals.

I was probably comfortable with that knowledge, though, and whilst I would continue working hard and improving my best times, it would not be to the detriment of everything else. There was more to life than endlessly ploughing up and down highly anonymous pools throughout the Midlands, and I did not want to miss out on other aspects of life.

In my mind, though, I really wanted to improve my water polo. That was my game, and I enjoyed playing immensely. Dad had started a Halesowen team by now, and we were playing regularly in the lower Birmingham leagues with some success.

Over the next few years, I relished going to the English Schools Championships each Autumn. I spent a few days in Cardiff, Cambridge, and Leeds, enjoying the competition without setting the aquatic world on fire. I became the county champion and record holder for several strokes and distances, but it was very much a matter of being a big fish in a small pool. The peak of my swimming success later was becoming an English Universities Champion frequently, but only in relays, and representing the English Universities in a UK-wide competition. The latter event was on Grandstand on the BBC, where viewers might have seen me some distance behind the future Mexico Olympic silver medallist Martyn Woodroffe in the 400m Individual Medley.

About this time, we all, parents included, dropped out of attending Long Lane Methodist Chapel. I don't remember any discussions about it, but Sunday worship was no longer in our lives. I don't recall any meaningful conversations about anything in any way contentious at home. Like when I first brought it up at Cheadle, the rule was,

"No talking at the tea table."

And that was that.

***

Dad always came home for lunch, something he did throughout his long post office career. Now we boys all had school meals. Mum assumed this to be our main meal of the day. Tea was basically bread and jam and cakes. As I was training hard and very active and school meals notoriously stingy, I was often hungry and fancied something more for tea, something savoury, if only a couple of eggs on toast or some baked beans, but when I tried to raise the issue with Mum, I got nowhere.

I resorted to going to lunch with several girls I knew who ate like sparrows and had them supplement my calorific intake.

The December Halesowen SC gala came around. Again, I won several events, and my brothers were now becoming competitive in their age group events and picked up some silverware.

That Christmas, in 1964, Dad wangled me a job as a Temporary Christmas worker at the Post Office. They had set the minimum age for such employment at eighteen, but he could secure me some paid employment with a bit of subterfuge. I was only fifteen, but I enjoyed meeting up with young University students also working hard to supplement their grants, and it was a fun, buzzy atmosphere. The camaraderie was great as we met up for a festive turkey sandwich late lunch in the café next to the sorting office after a hard few hours delivering Christmas mail.

The money was quite a bonus as I worked long hours from when school broke up until Christmas Eve, and I felt pretty wealthy on opening my pay packet. I earmarked the cash for more LPs and even some trendier casual clothes to enhance my hopefully cool image.

The Animals had recently released an album that was first on my list for record purchases, and I also picked up 'Beatles for Sale' fresh off the Christmas presses.

I remember at around that time also buying some fashionable chisel-toed shoes that would not have met with Dad's approval. Mum was fine with them and could understand my motivation, but Dad would have had a bit of a fit. So I resorted to hiding them in the outside lean-to area and had to change into them discretely to avoid him making derogatory comments.

As well as the money, though, the entire experience of the hard work, sorting and delivering mail, and the camaraderie amongst all the young students and the regular full-time staff was most enjoyable. I knew quite a few full-time postmen by now and had turned out a few times to guest for their casual football team.

Back at school in January, the focus on every subject was finishing the topics not already covered in the syllabus. We then embarked on a dreary programme of revision in readiness for what staff and pupils alike construed as being the most critical event in our lives. 'O' level examinations. The consensus seemed like that to me, anyway.

My approach was a bit more circumspect, and I didn't believe the hyperbole about the importance of these forthcoming examinations. Undoubtedly, I would work hard at my revision, but what would be would be. Comfortable with my grasp of the various concepts, I felt I had an excellent technique for revision, which entailed crystallising subjects down to just key bullet points written on small index cards. Extensive use of mnemonics, which would trigger the memory (hopefully) of complete sections of study, always helped me. U MAD CAP FAG was one of these, which I have committed to memory now for over fifty-five years. I don't have a clue what it stands for now, but that group of ten letters could unlock a whole subject at one stage.

***

A significant event occurred that January in the United Kingdom with the death of probably the most remarkable British Statesman of the twentieth century, Sir Winston Churchill, at ninety-one.

A State funeral, customarily reserved for royals and planned for a way back in 1953, was held in his honour and television coverage was extensive. They finally lay the war leader and politician to rest in the family plot at the small country church in Bladon, Oxfordshire.

When I was in the Lower Sixth, the following year, there was a school trip to visit Blenheim Palace, which included a quick visit to the Bladon churchyard. The simple and tranquil ambience of the country setting, particularly when placed alongside the grandiose magnificence and enormous scale of the family seat, quite took me.

In February, we had mock examinations. I did a bit of revision, but did not fret over things too much. My results were ok, and I did not expect any problems with the real thing a few months later.

By around this time, I had a girlfriend, the same age as me, Ruth, who I had met through swimming and lived in Sedgley, the other side of Dudley. Our parents had met each other as they officiated at various Midlands swimming events and we saw each other regularly training and competing. We also had reciprocal visits and meals in our respective homes, as our parents had become friendly. I think Mum and Dad appreciated I was

133

growing up, and at least they were aware of what I was getting up to and could monitor things, at least from a distance.

Another aspect of growing up centred around playing men's water polo. With a team put together by Dad (who was also still playing for Stourbridge), Halesowen were doing well in the leagues, and I was becoming more and more proficient and scoring most of the team's goals, although I was the youngest player around.

They held games weekday evenings throughout Greater Birmingham, often in old Victorian swimming baths, followed by after-match receptions held in the upstairs rooms of similarly old and very atmospheric pubs. We enjoyed refreshments such as cheese and onion rolls, slices of traditional Black Country black pudding and raw onion, washed down with jugs of bitter ale.

It just seemed natural to accept the proffered beer as I chatted to opposition players. They gave us half-pint beer mugs, and the hosts would regularly come around and top up empty glasses. While talking, I would see Dad, equally engrossed in conversation, checking my consumption out of the corner of my eye. Immediately registering what this was all about, I understood that the drinking was allowable as long as it did not become excessive. And I did not become detrimentally affected by my intake.

Careful never to give Dad any reason to admonish me, I believe my drinking apprenticeship in those upstairs rooms in old Victorian pubs stood me in excellent stead. Soon I could quaff with the best, and remain in proper order.

At school, I found the constant revision and emphasis on the upcoming exams quite tedious and became a little bored with the entire process. With the absence of our primary history teacher for some time due to illness, I found the replacement lessons given by the elderly deputy headmistress quite refreshing.

It would appear she spent her summers touring around Greece in the company of such luminaries as Sir Mortimer Wheeler, an eminent archaeologist who was often on television. Her lessons comprised the class looking at her holiday slides of ruined statues and temples and hearing her anecdotes about the colourful people she had met on the trip. She also had an abundance of tales about ancient Greek history, nothing to do with our current syllabus. But a little light relief all the same.

When we broke up for half term, we would return to take our exams throughout June. They would be over by the end of the month, so I was looking forward to being able to enjoy a long summer holiday period lasting some nine weeks when this traumatic time was past. Getting the exams over and done with was my focus.

We spent the holiday week at Cai Bach, New Quay as we frequently did, camping in our regular field. One of the first things I needed to do this holiday was to 'wear in' my new Levi jeans. I had bought a pair just before the holiday, and in those days, they did not come pre-washed, pre-shrunk or 'distressed'. We bought them one size too large and shrunk them to fit. People used to resort to sitting in the bath wearing them initially to soften them up, fade them, and ensure they were comfortable and wearable.

When first bought, they would stand up on their own, being so thick and heavy. I planned to put the jeans on and go swimming in the sea wearing them. It was quite an effort to achieve the required effect, but it was worth it.

I have always been loyal to the Levis brand and have owned no other denim wear to this day.

After sorting my jeans out, I needed to revise to ensure I was as prepared as possible for the exams. But I also wanted to enjoy our family beach holiday.

As usual, I was in my separate tent and woke quite early each day, read through all my edited card index notes for a specific subject each day, and then quietly got up and headed through the woods to the beach.

Once on the lovely peaceful beach, I walked around to New Quay along the shoreline, reciting key points to myself and ensuring I knew what all the mnemonic triggers meant. By the time I had reached the picturesque harbour and then returned, I could mentally compartmentalise that subject and put it to bed for the rest of the week. I could then enjoy my breakfast, as the walk would have given me an appetite. We would then spend the rest of the day involved in all our usual family holiday activities.

Coincidentally my girlfriend at the time (I had moved on from Ruth of Sedgeley), a pretty and petite blonde girl of a Welsh background, Anwyn, who had only recently joined the school from a few miles away closer to Birmingham, was holidaying in the area with her parents. We met up a couple of times, and then her dad surprised me by inviting me over to their caravan, saying he would cook a meal for us.

A couple of months before, our first date was when I took her to the Odeon cinema in the city centre to watch the highly acclaimed Kubrick film Dr Strangelove, starring Peter Sellers. They purported it to be a black comedy satirising the Cold War, but I found it weird. It was in black and white for a start. I felt short-changed forking out a reasonably hefty figure for two prime seats and not even getting colour. The other thing was that I was not wearing my glasses, so the screen was fuzzy and, to be fair, my focus was not primarily on the movie.

Mr Griffiths, Anwyn's dad, was an art teacher and an excellent cook. He had produced a beautifully designed and hand-illustrated menu and cooked up a traditional Welsh meal involving laverbread (seaweed) as a starter, Welsh lamb and Pembrokeshire new potatoes. My first experience of the laverbread served with a poached egg, was quite acceptable. Fishy flavoured spinach really, which he must have got hold of around New Quay harbour.

When he served the main course, with the cold dessert left on a side table, he and his wife left saying they were going for a walk for an hour. Excellently tactful.

Our liaison did not last many more weeks after this holiday. There was no dramatic falling out, just perhaps a realisation that we were different people.

Anwyn was very arty (given her dad's background, this was not surprising), musical (she had a sweet voice and played the guitar), and a thespian. She took the lead role of Katherina in the school production of Shakespeare's *'Taming of the Shrew'*, playing opposite Stephen Bill's Petruchio. The latter was an excellent actor who studied at RADA and had a successful career as a stage television and film actor and then focussed on his playwriting.

Anwyn preferred this environment, mixing with fellow thespians, musicians and artists, and was more cerebral than me. I was probably a happy-go-lucky, fun-loving Jock, and perhaps not serious-minded enough for her.

A little further down the line, Derek picked up the baton, and they became an item, at least until we all finished school.

When the exams came, I felt I did as well as I could in all the subjects. The only cause for concern was French, where I thought I might scrape a pass but probably not. I was pretty confident that I would secure the five decent passes needed to get into the Sixth form, which was the main thing.

While still too young to work officially at the post office, Dad was short-staffed postal delivery staff-wise, so he offered me a full-time job over this long holiday time. It meant clocking in for work at 5.30 am six days a week, but the plus side was that I was finished for the day at 1 pm.

I was mainly ok with getting up and walking a couple of miles into Blackheath. One day, however, I overslept and had to run down Long Lane to avoid being late. This early morning activity aroused the local constabulary's suspicions. Driving their patrol car, they saw me running ahead of them, switched on the blues and twos and pulled me over. The potential arrest for suspicion of burglary was worrying, but they kindly gave me a lift for the rest of the journey when I had the chance to explain the circumstances.

I loved the job as I was my own boss, with my designated delivery round. First, I had to collect all the mail for my 'walk', sort it, bundle it, and pack it in my large canvas bag, ready for delivery. We could not go out onto the streets until at least 7 am, so we often had a few minutes spare to have a coffee and a chat before going out on the first round.

I treated the job as a challenge, looking to improve my time to complete the round as fast as possible and deliver my post efficiently. Early on, this desire to complete my round quickly led to a couple of complaints from members of the public not taking kindly to me, jumping over hedges or cutting across front lawns. One day back at the sorting office, feeling quite pleased with my record time, a supervisor took me to one side and showed me a list of about four or five minor complaints he had received. My delivery approach had to be changed from that time forward, with former shortcuts banned.

We returned to New Quay for our family holidays again that summer, and I found that coincidentally, a group of friends had booked into the caravan park just up the bay from us at the same time. This occurrence was not unusual because this stretch of the Welsh coastline was very popular with people from the West Midlands.

It was an additional welcome element to have some schoolmates around, and we would all meet up at our lovely quiet area of the beach where the stream flowed into the sea. There was an abundance of large smooth boulders to sit on and lots of bone-dry driftwood, and in the early evening, after our usual beach activities, we would build a fire out of the driftwood.

We then cooked basic sausages and burgers and drank flagons of cider. Eating and drinking all evening, we listened to music on the radio before crashing out directly on the beach in our sleeping bags in the early hours of the morning. Mum, Dad and my brothers would return to our campsite somewhat earlier.

A transistor radio tuned to one of the pirate radio stations provided a fantastic musical soundtrack. We were living through a revolutionary period in the history of popular culture. The Rolling Stones 'Satisfaction' was a great hit that summer, but I particularly loved the single released earlier in the year, 'The Last Time'. There were lots of Beatles tracks in the charts, Motown was there with the Four Tops, The Byrds made a jangly version of a Dylan song, 'Mr Tambourine Man,' which was very popular, and the Beach Boys, the Yardbirds 'For Your Love' and Sonny and Cher's 'I Got You Babe' were all given regular airtime.

It was a magical time in my life as I looked forward to the freer, more grown-up, Sixth Form regime which would start in a month's time. There was also the prospect of being a student for three more years beyond that. The world was my lobster.

The exam results came out sometime towards the end of August, and I was happy enough with seven decent 'O' level passes and a twinge of disappointment with just failing French.

CHAPTER 13

READY FOR SIXTH FORM LIFE

Soon after getting my grades, I received a letter from the headteacher summoning me to his house. This was within the school grounds, but hidden up a grand drive and screened by dense laurels. The Head invited all the pupils who had taken the 'O' level examinations to meet with him on a one-to-one basis to discuss our prospects for the future.

Old Emmett congratulated me on what he said was a commendable achievement. The results, he told me, would stand me in excellent stead for a successful study period in the sixth form, leading hopefully to a good university placement.

I had not met with the old chap, white of hair and moustache and pink of visage, face to face, since about eighteen months earlier. On this earlier occasion, he caught me and four others red-handed as he walked down his drive from lunch. We were snowballing, which he had expressly forbidden in that morning's assembly.

When we reported to his office as required, he was pacing up and down, quite apoplectic with rage. We had all chosen to disregard his precise command not to indulge in snow fights. He was fingering the end of his cane distractedly and constantly giving the weapon a swish as he laid into us verbally before doing so physically. With six of the best for us all.

Now, at this meeting, he was initially pretty benign, but when I answered which university I had in mind, I thought I was in for a repeat performance.

"I would like to go to Loughborough College to study PE, sir," I answered.

"With these 'O' level results and a decent performance in the Sixth form, of which I know you are well capable, you could get into any of the red bricks. Why do you want to set your stall so low?" He was referring to the tier of established universities just below the Oxbridge level.

"I don't think I am, sir. Loughborough is the best PE College in the country, possibly in the world."

"Hmmph. It is still just a Teacher Training College. You could do so much better. Bristol, Nottingham, Manchester, Birmingham, Leeds, Durham, Sheffield. Any of them."

I stood my ground, and there was a brief chat about what subjects I would take at 'A' level. By then, he had appeared to lose interest in me, and he dismissed me from his presence with a disappointed wave of the arm.

***

At the end of the summer, with my post office savings account looking relatively healthy, I took myself off to Harry Fenton's menswear shop, up Hagley Road. And blew a chunk of hard-earned cash on an Italian-style suit with fabric-covered buttons.

The Harry Fenton chain was renowned as the place where the Mods got their threads. I would not claim to be a fully paid-up member of the cool parka-wearing Lambretta-riding sub-culture that had emerged over the last couple of years. However, I realised the need to pay attention to my appearance and image. I also liked the music they favoured, like the Yardbirds, the Small Faces and the Who, so I was a sort of semi-mod.

The suit became my default 'cool dude' wear for teenage house parties, which were becoming more and more common. They held these with the agreement of liberal-minded parents, or occasionally not. While loving a party, Mum and Dad would not have sanctioned such adult-free assemblies, and I would not have dreamed of suggesting we hold one at Oak Tree Crescent.

There were parties, however, elsewhere most weekends with lots of cider, cheap wine, the surreptitious raiding of cocktail cabinets, lots of fantastic music, dancing and other teenage activities.

My choice of 'A' level subjects to study gave me some cause for thought. There were some meetings at school with teachers to discuss different options. I would have liked to take biology, but as I had only studied general science (in which I gained a top grade) at 'O' level, this was not permissible. Although apparently, I could take physics, which did not seem logical to me.

The maths teacher, Mrs Waller, was keen on me studying her subject and suggested I also take physics. She was a strong character and quite persuasive. I wanted to take geography, so I finally settled on maths, physics, geography and general studies and was heading off to the Lower Sixth (Science).

September came around, and we became Sixth Formers. This meant we had our common room with tea and coffee-making facilities, sofas and armchairs, and study tables and chairs. There were some free periods programmed into the week for private study, so the whole regime appeared much more civilised. Uniforms were also no longer required, which was quite liberating.

My chosen subjects, though, were causing me some concern. It soon became obvious it was a big mistake being persuaded to take physics not having studied the subject at 'O' level. I did not have the background knowledge and was out of my depth from day one. At least I recognised this and went straight away to the teacher to explain my feelings and also had a chat with the sixth form tutor.

The outcome was that I dropped physics and opted for economics. I took to this subject readily and the master in charge helped considerably. All the pupils knew him as Stretch because he was six foot seven; he gave me some personal tuition to enable me to catch up with the rest of the class. I clearly remember being in a one-on-one session with him scrawling and highlighting continuously so that it was a dominant, thick, black name on the page by the end of proceedings. JOHN MAYNARD KEYNES. Keynes, according to Stretch (and many others, to be fair), was the founding father of British Economics, and I should follow his teachings. Thus, I have always advocated Keynesian Economics, a school of thought that seems to have innumerable disciples even today. Essential elements include advocating increased government spending in a recession and exercising restraint in a booming economy, preventing increases in demand which spur inflation.

Lower sixth form life was relatively easy-going, and often in free periods at our home base, we would sit, chat, drink coffee, and listen to music on the radio. Or else put on some records. Two of the girls were quite good on acoustic guitar and would also play their versions of some Dylan tunes.

I very much liked Dylan's powerful, thought-provoking and poetic songs, but was not hugely appreciative of his nasal delivery. He was not the world's greatest singer. However, that autumn, Joan Baez, a lady not unknown to the American troubadour, brought out a superb album called 'Farewell Angelina', including many Bob Dylan tunes.

The title track, a Dylan song, was an extraordinary, hauntingly beautiful, crystal clear rendition. This very much endeared me to her as a performer and as an interpreter of some of Dylan's great songs. I bought the album and then added about three or four more of her LP records to my collection.

Dylan had caused some controversy earlier in the year by playing electric guitar at the Newport Folk Festival, leading many of the folk fraternity to boo his performance. I was ambivalent about this; acoustic or electric, I didn't mind. His songs were great, but I probably preferred (this changed later) to hear Joan Baez and others like the Byrds playing his tunes.

One of the young sixth-form guitarists could produce a commendable interpretation of 'Farewell, Angelina'. And then a little later, when the Beatles brought out 'Rubber Soul', she added 'Norwegian Wood' and 'Michelle' to her repertoire.

I bought 'Rubber Soul' straight away on its release, as many thousands of others did. Beatlemania had hit the USA, and the Beatles had broken the all-time concert attendance records. 55,000 turned out to see them at Shea Stadium that summer, and for a period, they could do no wrong.

Having seen television footage of the American stadium concert, I realised it was virtually impossible to hear the 'fab four'. The constant piercing screaming from the predominantly young female audience spoiled it for me. To my mind, it would not have been a great concert to attend.

Another local band emerging on the music scene significantly affected Derek, me and the rest of our gang, at the end of 1965. With the single 'Keep on Running', the Spencer Davis Group, a

Birmingham-based four-piece, broke through in the popular music world of the day. With the prodigiously talented Steve Winwood on vocals, guitar and organ, the band produced a sound with which to be reckoned. The younger Winwood (Muff Winwood, who was to become a hugely successful producer, was also in the band) had an incredibly evocative, bluesy voice, reminiscent of Ray Charles. His wonderful playing of the distinctive-sounding Hammond organ was sublime. The Spencer Davis Group hooked us from the outset.

The Christmas period was a whirl of Post Office work, house parties and the usual swimming training, competitions and water polo matches. Hard, but lucrative work, physical effort in the swimming pool and the gym, and hedonism were a vibrant mix that seemed to suit my personality. It is often said that 'school days are the best years of your life'. While I would not necessarily totally concur with that sentiment, there was no doubt I was having a great time.

The British music scene was taking the world by storm in early 1966. The Animals, The Searchers, Manfred Mann, The Hollies, The Who and The Kinks were all to the fore. However, on top of the pile were The Rolling Stones and, of course, The Beatles. It was March this year that John Lennon said in the Press, "We're more popular than Jesus now; I don't know what will go first. Rock 'n' roll or Christianity."

The establishment did not receive this statement particularly well. The perception taken by the media was that it was very arrogant.

***

Prime Minister Harold Wilson called a snap election at the end of March. This decision reaped dividends when the Labour Party emerged with a majority in the Commons of nearly a hundred seats.

My seventeenth birthday rolled around in April. I had had a perfect day on the Saturday directly before the Sunday of my birthday. I broke the county backstroke record and then went to an open house somewhere in Halesowen in the evening, which I regarded as my birthday party.

Parties were often a bit of a hit-or-miss affair, but this one ticked all the boxes. I remember The Lovin' Spoonful's song

'What a Day for a Daydream', which was top of the charts being given a lot of spins. It was a bright, optimistic song and caught the mood just right. It was a beautiful spring evening, and everybody seemed to be in excellent humour, singing, dancing, chatting and drinking. The probable reason was, as it was mostly a lower Sixth crowd, no significant exams were coming up, and a long summer holiday was in prospect.

***

Around a month later, on the 6th of May, to be exact, a gruesome news story that had been highly prominent in the press reached its conclusion. The jury found 'Moors Murderers' Ian Brady and Myra Hindley guilty of the most despicable acts of sexual perversion, torture, and murder. They buried five innocent youngsters in shallow graves on Saddleworth Moor. The news coverage had been intense, and the world's press was in attendance in vast numbers as the trial reached its conclusion. The story had played out in horrific detail over the previous couple of years since the discovery of a child's remains on the bleak moors above Manchester.

I read a lot of the press coverage (there were always newspapers in the common room). It was heart-rending. They were unbelievably callous and evil people, and I could not fathom their thought processes. Absolutely incomprehensible and thoroughly heinous behaviour.

The guilty verdicts led to the defendants being handed concurrent life sentences, and neither was to see the outside world again. The Press called Hindley the 'most evil woman in Britain', whilst the presiding Judge described the pair as "two sadistic killers of the utmost depravity".

***

We decamped to New Quay again at the end of May and enjoyed our regular Whit week break. Dad chose the holiday week (again) to let us know the GPO had offered a further promotion and we would move to Rugby in Warwickshire. This was about fifty miles east and south of Halesowen. My brothers would start a new school in the autumn. They did not look over pleased about this potential upheaval, remembering the episodes of bullying and general unpleasantness accompanying their previous school changes.

Dad pre-empted my concerns about moving halfway through my 'A' levels when he explained he had arranged for me to stay with Mrs Rea. Mrs Rea, a pleasant widow who lived alone two doors down the crescent, had agreed to take me in as a lodger. This would enable me to complete my studies at Halesowen Grammar. She would feed me and do my washing, so that was all in hand. I was happy with this arrangement as effectively, it meant I was leaving home (or the family was leaving me) and I was living an independent student life a year before schedule.

This week on our New Quay holiday, I found a second Welsh girlfriend, a lovely, tall, dark-haired girl. She lived conveniently in a tiny hamlet on the main road about half a mile from where we camped. She was the complete opposite physically of Anwyn.

I bumped into Ruth at the village shop, and we started chatting, and one thing led to another. My second Ruth in just a short dating career. She was a year younger than me and was keen to get away from rural Wales and go to a teacher training college in England. We spent a lot of time on the beach with my family and frequently walked over to New Quay, chatting, drinking coffee, and enjoying each other's company. Mum and Ruth got on very well together, which was good to see.

This new relationship would have to work at a distance. It did for a couple of years, as we still went to Wales for holidays. I even saw her for a while when she went to a teacher training college at Scraptoft outside Leicester a couple of years later.

The farmer had by now turned the original Cei Bach camping field of our earlier days into a proper site. He obviously realised that Dad had had a good idea all those years before and there was more revenue from selling camping plots to Midlanders than raising cattle.

Dad would take up his new position in the summer and would hopefully have a new family home for Mum and the boys to move into before the end of the school holidays. This would enable them to start their new school in the autumn term.

Another memory of that holiday was taking a trip up the coast to the pretty harbour town of Aberaeron as I had seen a poster advertising a harbour sports day. This included some swimming races, and I persuaded Dad to take us. There was quite a carnival atmosphere throughout the place, and they had set a swimming course up in the harbour. I signed up for the Boys' and the Senior Mens' freestyle events. I won them both, diving from a floating platform before tackling the cross-harbour course and dealing with, unusual for me in a swimming race, the waves and murky, salt water.

***

The release of the Spencer Davis Group's 'Second Album' was in the early part of the new year. I was reasonably flush with my earnings, so I could readily add it to my collection. Our group then unearthed details of their forthcoming live gigs in small venues throughout the Greater Birmingham area.

One such performance in the early summer saw them topping the bill at a nondescript venue in the middle of the Black Country somewhere. Support was from a Wolverhampton band called the Californians. I was not even really aware there was a support act. However, this group played brilliant covers of the Beach Boys' hits and those of other West Coast performers. Their set included an exceptional rendition of 'Good Vibrations', which must have been very difficult to perform live. I distinctly remember being completely in awe of their authentic sound and stagecraft.

After this excellent appetiser and a couple of interval pints, it was the turn of the Steve Winwood-led outfit to provide some mesmeric music. This guy was just a year older than us. Unbelievable. As part of the Birmingham blues-rock scene, he had backed luminaries such as Muddy Waters, John Lee Hooker, BB King, Howlin' Wolf, Chuck Berry and Bo Diddley on guitar, piano, Hammond organ and vocals on their UK tours. He had a most impressive c.v., even at eighteen.

Winwood and his colleagues did not disappoint and played a fantastic set. It was such a joyous and memorable occasion, and I knew that going to live music events was something I would always do from then on. The Spencer Davis event was probably the first real gig I attended. But we followed it by seeing the Hollies at Birmingham University later that summer and other lesser-known local cover bands around our West Midlands home area.

***

On top of all the family disturbance over the summer with Dad about to start his new job and them both embarking on house

146

hunting, it was not a good time for Dad to succumb to a bout of jaundice. This laid him low for a couple of weeks or longer. Looking sallow and weak, it confined him to his bed, which I found quite shocking. Dad had always been in robust health, and I don't remember him even having colds or flu.

For our major summer holiday that year, Dad, still in recovery and probably not wanting the hassle and physical work involved with camping, decided on a caravan holiday for us. The family duly decamped to Woolacombe in Devon.

Although the weather was mixed, we had a decent enough time, to put it mildly. We boys enjoyed surfing but made sure we kept within the flags as the rip tides on this beach were quite notorious. We just had plywood bodyboards with curved ends, which we bought locally and cheaply.

Dad spent most of his time in a deckchair, most unlike him, as he continued his slow progress to regaining full fitness. However, one day, he went for a bit of a paddle and was only around knee-deep in the surf when he fell into one of the many deep holes caused by the wave action. He struggled to get up. Halfway up, Dad couldn't handle the fierce back tow and was immediately down again. The strong currents brought him down another couple of times. We, a few yards down the beach, realised he was in trouble and rushed to pull him out of the swirling white waters.

He was very weak with the effort of fighting the waves, and he needed all the help he could get to reach the safety of the beach. To see my fit, vigorous dad, such a powerful swimmer struggling to handle the conditions, shocked me. It made me realise how debilitating his illness had been and how fragile life can be. It was at least a month before we were all relieved to see him back to full strength.

That Woolacombe holiday was in the week of our greatest-ever football World Cup success, culminating in the 4-2 extra-time victory over the Germans.

Amazingly, we did not get to see this massive event on television and I think the day passed with none of us even being aware they had screened it. Maybe we got to hear the score on the radio.

I had followed the earlier rounds and the team's progress closely, with games against Argentina and the semi-final against Portugal sticking in my memory. So, to miss the final seemed a bit off.

***

I was home after the holidays for a short while before I went to a Midlands Swimming Squad training camp. This was a residential training week held at the prestigious Crystal Palace National Recreation Centre in SE London.

The week turned out to be a highly intensive programme of two or three pool sessions a day and some land conditioning in the gym. I kept a training log and totted up that we swam over 40,000 yards that week – over twenty-two miles.

We were all very fit, but the week was physically challenging. We still had the energy, however, to be diving in and out of each other's rooms in the evenings after dinner for extracurricular activities. Housed in the purpose-built residential accommodation, we had to race up and down the fire escape to avoid detection by the patrolling chaperones. It was safe to say we proved more than a match for them.

CHAPTER 14

HOME WITH MRS REA

Moving into Mrs Rea's, a couple of doors further down Oak Tree Crescent, towards the end of the holidays, I just took a pile of clothes, a bunch of LPs and my trusty record player. Mrs Rea had allocated me a sizeable double back bedroom to use. This room became my bed-sit. Set up as a student-style studio suitable for doing my schoolwork and relaxing to read and listen to music. She had given me an armchair and a coffee table, which I placed in the bay window. This looked out over the mature and well stocked back garden. I also as had a desk and chair for my studies.

By this time, I was reading the novels of John Steinbeck. I would often spend time comfortably ensconced in the armchair, losing myself in the depression years in the USA and savouring Steinbeck's wonderfully evocative descriptions.

Mrs Rea appreciated having me around, not that we spent much time together, but it just meant that she was not rattling around in the house alone. Her daughter Kathryn, two or three years older than me, had moved up to Scotland to university after leaving Halesowen Grammar, and she admitted she missed her. Kath had driven up north in her new white mini, of which I was envious. The registration was FRE 361B – another bit of useless information my mind has always kept locked in for unfathomable reasons.

I wanted a car but, as yet, had not even started learning to drive. The logistics were a little challenging to fit driving lessons in, so I decided I would wait until the following summer when I had finished school.

A couple of weeks later, Derek and I hitchhiked on a free Saturday over to Rugby as I wanted to check out where my family had moved to.

We took the bus across Birmingham, right out to the city's eastern edge, close to the airport, and thumbed for a lift. I had done a fair bit of hitching, just locally to meet up with friends, and found it an effective way of getting around. It seemed acceptable in those days and people did not seem to look down on the practice, as they would in later times.

We got to Rugby in two or three lifts. I only had a vague understanding of where exactly my parents had moved to. Looking around when our last lift dropped us off on the outskirts of the town, I said to Derek,

"I think it is down here."

"What do you mean, you think it is down here? Don't you know where you live?" He replied, quite amazed.

"Not really. I've never been before."

After about a mile of walking, I shouted,

"That's it. Ratliffe Road, just off Shakespeare Gardens."

It was good to catch up with the family, who all knew Derek as he had been on holiday with us in the past. The house was a step up from Halesowen, a modern three-bedroom detached place with a sizeable garden and a detached garage. Mum, particularly, seemed happy with the set-up and said,

"All the neighbours are lovely John. It is a smashing place."

Derek took great delight when we were back at school recounting the story:

"He didn't even know where he bloody lived!"

Mrs Rea was happy for me to go downstairs and watch television in her lounge. But I was more comfortable after my evening meal, perhaps after seeing the news, retreating to my bedsit. Adapting to student life came easily to me. Enjoying making my own decisions about when I came and went, and not really having to answer to anyone, was I felt cathartic. There was a certain amount of schoolwork to cover. However, with free periods at school, I could achieve a lot during the regular school day. Training and playing commitments for swimming and polo took up a fair amount of my time. The weekends were about socialising and swimming galas. At seventeen, I had the key to the door.

Dropping physics the previous year was a good option. But I found that this affected my maths. The maths 'A' level course we studied was in two sections, pure and applied maths. The former I could handle and even enjoyed with its advanced algebra and calculus and concepts like differentiation and integration, but the applied form was a different story. Closely allied to physics and requiring in-depth knowledge of that subject to make any sense, applied maths was a struggle for me. After persevering for an entire year, it became apparent that I would struggle to pass A-level maths. Speaking to teachers, we decided to drop maths. History would take its place, and I would start studying from the new autumn term. Everyone could see the logic in this course of action.

Again, some one-to-one tuition enabled me to catch up. A new young woman teacher taught me and allowed me to use her university notes, which was a tremendous bonus. Being a year behind would affect my potential mark, so I focused on some critical elements of the syllabus and made a strategic decision to miss out on some topics. I would therefore go into the exam effectively with one hand behind my back, but it was a risk I was happy to take.

The exams were a three-hour test requiring four essay questions to be answered. When the day came around, it delighted me to scan the paper and see two topics which I knew very well on the list of questions. With a third, my knowledge was passable. For my fourth choice, whilst my grasp of the arguments might be a little sketchy, I knew enough salient points to pick up a few marks. It all turned out fine in the end.

Early into the new term and getting used to life in the Middle Sixth, the entire country was sad to see the awful catastrophe unfolding on television in South Wales. After a lengthy period of heavy rain, a colliery spoil tip slipped down the mountainside at Aberfan, close to Merthyr Tydfil. One hundred and forty-four people died as the coal waste slurry flowed down the slope to engulf a primary school. One hundred and sixteen of the disaster victims were young children, and the television pictures of the rescue attempts in the grim, grey drizzle were indeed heart-rending.

The nation was in shock for some time after this cruel event.

That November, having submitted my application some months previously, I received a letter saying they had granted me an interview at Loughborough. This was the news I had been waiting for.

Travelling up to Loughborough by train, I was to be ready for a formal academic interview and a practical assessment. Staff would look at basic skill levels and motor coordination to judge whether I was the right material to become a PE teacher.

We were required to perform a standing long jump and a vertical jump, both excellent indicators of athletic ability, pull-ups, press-ups, forward and backward rolls, a rope climb, and other physical tests. We were all then involved with catching, throwing, trapping and passing various balls thrown in our direction as we jogged around the gym.

I went flying up the rope climb arms only, something I regularly did in my circuit training. A big broad Scotsman whom I had previously spoken to, probably weighing close to eighteen stone, stood at the bottom proclaiming in a thick Kirkcaldy accent (Kerrkoddy was how he pronounced his hometown),

"I canna dooit. I canna cleemit. Soory."

This failure on the rope climb didn't hold him back, though. Dave Sellar soon became the first team tighthead prop and was in my geography group for the next three years.

The academic interview covered sporting abilities, achievements and aspirations, hobbies, reading, and academic studies. The interviewer asked questions about my 'O' level results and confirmed my seven good grades, including English and Maths, had already given me the minimum entry requirements for Loughborough. He then asked what my expected marks at 'A' level would be. I told the admissions officer they had predicted I would achieve two As and two Cs, and he made some scribbles on his notepad. He also seemed to note my affection for Steinbeck's writing positively.

Two or three weeks later, I received a formal offer for the following September intake, conditional on obtaining one A-level pass. Immediately, this put a different perspective on how I would approach my final year in the Sixth form.

I could cruise and still get to my dream place of further education. We were well ahead of the game in terms of the geography syllabus. Economics I was enjoying, and again we had covered the bulk of the curriculum topics. I was comfortable with what I was aiming to do with history, and the general studies paper was about comprehension and common sense more than anything else. There were sections of French and Latin which may prove tough, but I was not concerned.

I thought to myself, with some relief, that I could look forward to the rest of the academic year without undue anxiety. It was probably the offer I was expecting, but a relief nevertheless. Many of my friends were already stressing about achieving the required grades for their chosen tertiary education places, but I felt fortunate.

I celebrated the news of my offer by acquiring the Spencer Davis Group's recent release, aptly titled 'Autumn 66.'

The album was played endlessly in my room until I knew every nuance of Steve Winwood's emotional bluesy renditions. The classic 'Nobody loves you when you are down and out' was my big favourite, and still is after all this time. Also, I loved 'Georgia', and 'When a Man Loves a Woman,' not even realising the latter was a Percy Sledge cover.

Life at Mrs Rea's was most acceptable. She introduced me to dishes from her native North East like pan haggerty, panacalty, boiled ham and pease pudding and stottie cakes. I was happy to eat anything. She would have given a fussy eater short shrift.

I was a bit taken aback once when she served up a dish essentially of roasted chicory leaves with a couple of rashers of bacon; I found the chicory quite bitter. Still, I got it down. Another time, she served up a dinner that consisted solely of Brussels sprouts in a cheese sauce. I think the housekeeping budget must have been low that day.

Also, this autumn, I received a formal invitation to attend the Midlands Under 18 water polo trials. This would determine whether I warranted being sent through to the National trials to be held at Crystal Palace in the new year.

A couple of weeks later, I got across to Walsall on a Sunday via several buses and a complicated journey to play in the trials. I don't think anyone else had had to make the journey by bus. The bulk of the players came from clubs playing in higher Midland Leagues and the National League, not turning out for lowly Halesowen. They had come in cars with coaches, team managers and parents, lobbying strongly for their inclusion in the list of selected triallists. I felt a little alone waiting on the poolside for my name to be called.

I must have played pretty well, though. It quickly became apparent that I would go to the National trials in the Spring from comments I had received from the officials.

***

Around this time at school, with, to my mind, studies under control and lots of free periods each week, I popped into school for morning registration as usual. But then, turn right around, head for the bus stop, and take a ride into central Birmingham.

I was happy to wander around the streets and become more familiar with the country's second city. I enjoyed walking around the old jewellery quarter and the central network of old canals. The canals played an essential part in the city's and the whole of the Black Country's growth. The entire region emerged as 'the world's workshop' at the start of the Industrial Revolution.

I visited some of the larger bookshops in the city. I bought a few McGraw Hill textbooks covering the academic study of Physical Education. Small second-hand record stores were also a regular haunt where I remember picking up some early Dylan singles and EPs.

Interested in the importance of diet for athletes, I went to health foods shops and bought seaweed tablets, wheat germ, and muesli.

I remembered having this fruit and grain-based cereal when I stayed at Aunty Hilda's in Stanmore when I was ten. She also had to buy it from health food places, I had noticed. The new power breakfasts would guarantee improved performances in the pool.

I was bunking off; it was true. But I justified my little adventures into Birmingham by convincing myself the expeditions were a part of my extended education. In the grand scheme of things, they would serve me better than lounging around the common room all day, pretending to be studying.

***

At the end of the term, I had been lodging with Mrs Rea for three months, barely seeing the rest of the family. So, I hitched over to Rugby for the Christmas holidays.

154

My brothers had continued using the second bedroom together, probably because they preferred it that way, having always shared a room. Also, Mum realised I would need somewhere to stay in the holidays. So, arriving at Ratliffe Road, I dumped my bag in the back bedroom and enjoyed catching up with the family news.

Mum said she would work at the post office over the Christmas period, doing some sorting shifts because she enjoyed the work and the camaraderie. It gave her a bit of pin money. She also found the friendly banter very enjoyable. Dad had sorted me out a job as well, and whilst I was still officially too young for the work, I was now a seasoned and experienced postal worker.

Dad said I could start early morning, sort and deliver the first and second rounds, which, with the volume of seasonal mail, would take me until four or five in the afternoon. I would then clock on again at 6 pm to work at the railway station, loading and unloading mail trains. He felt I would manage the double shifts, and I was sure it would be fine. The prospect of all that dosh was quite motivating!

Rugby Post Office was next to the busy mainline station, and mail trains frequently stopped through the night. With a few others, my job would be to empty all the relevant mailbags from the heaving baggage cars and load up the ones destined to go further south. We then drove a small tractor-like vehicle, towing the loaded trucks down to the sorting office.

The mail trains were on tight schedules and only stopped for ninety seconds, so the job of unloading and loading was quite a physical flurry of activity. The station workers soon learned to keep out of the way when our small student team entered the train. As soon as it stopped, we would board and hurl the canvas sacks onto the platform in double-quick time. We then lobbed in all the mail destined to go down south before the guard let out a long, shrill whistle. The train would continue its journey with a loud whoosh as they released the brakes.

Once we had taken the incoming mail down to the sorting office, we were free to sit around, chat and drink coffee before readying ourselves for the next train. It was good fun work.

Because of the sheer volume of Christmas mail destined for the South East, they offloaded sacks of letters for Surrey at

Rugby. They then sorted them in readiness for delivery down south. I often did a bit of sorting of this mail along with my other job. I still know the names of most of the towns and villages in the county. "Claygate?" would be shouted, and I would respond "Esher". Or the call would be, "Thames Ditton?" and the answer "Surbiton."

Dad thus programmed me to work about ten days of eighteen-hour stints. With Dad working flat out, Mum also doing a shift and me just making brief appearances at some ungodly hour, we were really like ships in the night. We barely saw each other as a family. My brothers had to fend for themselves, living on heated-up food Mum had left for them or else making cheese on toast for themselves.

On finishing reasonably early, around lunchtime on Christmas Eve, I was pleased to see snow falling and the town centre looking very festive. By now, I had made quite a few like-minded friends. With a few bob in our pockets, the sensible move was to do a little pub crawl around the town centre. Rugby, which I had not fully appreciated before, mainly because I didn't know the place, had so many decent pubs. We spent a most convivial afternoon and early evening in the bustling bars, bursting with bonhomie and festive cheer.

I eventually got home. The bracing walk through the snow sobered me up a degree. At least, to where I could disguise any residual inebriation well enough (I think) to convince Mum and Dad that I had just stopped off for a couple.

We had a wonderful family celebration that holiday season and I particularly remember Christmas morning, after unwrapping presents going around all the neighbours' houses for a drink or two. Mum and Dad had settled well into the local community, and they had already made some lovely friends.

One neighbour, Tony, held a senior position in a construction company, Gallifords, based in Coventry down the road. In chatting, he suggested he might have some casual holiday employment available once I became a student. I made a mental note.

We had been in correspondence with the relevant County Educational Authority and they showed me what funds I would receive. The authority paid all tuition, board and meals in full in those days, but additional funds allowed for 'incidental expenses' - presumably beer. This part of the grant was means-tested and took Dad's salary into account.

Because of this, I would get just a minimal additional sum, and in one letter from the Education people, they invited Dad to 'top this figure up'. Dad told me in no uncertain terms that I would get nothing further from the household budget. They would expect me to fend for myself in terms of additional financial needs. I felt this was perfectly fair, as I was more than capable of earning funds through my own endeavours.

Christmases took care of themselves, but doing some labouring in the construction industry with Tony, which paid well, would be more than helpful in the other holiday periods.

The morning drinks continued with Mum possibly taking on board a couple of sherries too many. She required some help in coordinating the various elements of the large-scale celebratory lunch to avoid a catastrophe, but it all came to the table eventually, as planned.

A few days at home over Christmas and the New Year, relaxing with no eighteen-hour days, binging on food and drink and far too much television was enjoyable. But in early January, I headed back to Halesowen for my final few months of schooling.

Dad dropped me at the Dunchurch junction on the A45. He said later that I was already getting into a vehicle before he had fully gone around the roundabout. Hitching was proving quite an efficient way of getting about.

School became the same mix of revision, writing essays and essentially truanting to discover more of Birmingham's hidden treasures.

We had some mock examinations early into the year, which I did not get excited about, doing minimal revision but pulling in some satisfactory marks.

I distinctly remember thinking that geography, a subject I had always loved, right since the days of Mr Young at Uttoxeter, was boring me. Throughout my schooling, I had enjoyed the subject, but here we had finished the syllabus, and the constant repetitive revision was dulling my senses. I did not find school very inspiring at this stage of my academic career.

Swimming and water polo were still going well. But while I thought I played well at the Crystal Palace National U18 trials, it did not look like I would achieve national honours this time around. Without this sounding like sour grapes, the big national league clubs lobbying strongly for their particular players held sway. Being a player from a backwater nobody had heard of did not help. Halesowen? Where's that?

A group of us visited the Old Halesonians Rugby Club out on the Hagley Road on the odd Saturdays. Post-match singing, beer drinking and general revelry produced a fantastic atmosphere, enhanced later when the DJ cranked up the music and played all the great new tunes around. 'Knock on Wood' by Eddie Floyd was popular. The Doors went down well and the more poppy Herman's Hermits and The Monkees. Eric Burdon and The Animals also had a new album out and they got a few plays.

Old Halesonians took a relaxed approach to the obvious underage drinking, which helped.

At Easter, I went back to Rugby and spent two weeks working for Tony on a couple of building sites in Coventry. It was good hard physical work, and it paid well as I was earning the same as the men, with the advantage of not having to pay any tax. I particularly enjoyed the challenge of keeping a couple of brickies going with bricks and 'muck' as a labourer. Racing up and down the scaffolding to make sure they had all they needed was a good, continuous workout.

Another thing on the site, as I was the youngster, was being sent to the mess room about ten minutes before any tea break. I had to get the kettle on and make everyone a cuppa. When the ten minutes were over (often extending to nearer twenty), I had to clear the cups away, wash up and give the place a tidy up. On cold, damp days, being inside, in the warmth, I did not perceive to be any kind of hardship.

Dad had by now taken himself along to the public baths at Rugby and introduced himself to the officials of the Rugby Seals Swimming Club one club night. The club was thriving and quite successful, boasting some talented and speedy swimmers, particularly amongst the girls. The venerable Regent Street base with old-fashioned changing cubicles lining the thirty-three and a third-yard pool was a decent enough facility, well maintained, freshly painted and spotless. Dad started working on establishing a water polo team at the club as soon as he became involved.

He also quickly got to know the dour old Scottish baths superintendent, a Mr Dick. When Dad learned that the town also had an outdoor pool that operated in the summer, he thought this was useful to know. He suggested to Mr Dick, at his next meeting with him, he had a son who would be available for lifeguarding duties if required. He hired me in advance.

***

I thought of Dad, leaving post office colleagues, family members and sporting associates in Boston when I was ten. He then forged new connections with co-workers, the church community, the swimming clubs and general friends and neighbours in Cheadle.

He then left all that behind to undergo the same process in Halesowen, becoming a hard-working stalwart of the town's new swimming club and making many new friends. Then, of course, he had to repeat the course of action in Rugby. Mum and Dad had many acquaintances, if the number of Christmas cards that came through the door every December was anything to go by. But in reality, they had moved on from friends at each place we lived and then had to build a new social network.

That process must have been difficult for them, but they never mentioned, let alone discussed the matter. It was what you did if you wanted to advance your career would be how Dad saw it.

The same was true of us boys. We made friends at all the different places we lived and the various schools we attended. Then had to leave them behind and go through the sometimes less than a straightforward process of building a new set of relationships. It would be wrong to say we had roots in a particular town or area. I remember pausing when asked in future years where I was from, having to think when framing an answer.

"The Midlands, really," was my standard answer.

I could tell the moves proved unsettling to my brothers, Robert and Richard, who had been through some difficult times gaining acceptance at new educational establishments and forming new friendships. They both suffered some bullying, although Robert had learned to box and was quite handy, which had the effect of deterring cowardly tormentors.

159

In a month or two, I was now thinking that I would leave Halesowen for the last time. During the college holiday, I would live in a town where I knew nobody. When they leave school and go away to college or university, most people would still maintain contact with old school chums in their home area during the holidays. That would not happen to me.

I kept in touch and saw Derek from time to time after leaving Birmingham and another good friend I had become closer to in the final years of school, Merv. However, the logistics of maintaining friendships over distance meant that the amount of contact rapidly dwindled.

***

At around that time, I felt that if I was to get on in the water polo world; I needed to leave Halesowen and join a top club. Halesowen would be impractical now, anyway. Reasonably close to Rugby was Leamington Spa, a National League team, so I persuaded Dad to take me there. He was happy to do so initially, but also thought it would be better all-round if I could drive myself. He started giving me some lessons.

I had a busy Easter holiday with the labouring work for Tony, some training and practice matches at Leamington (where I fitted in readily). I undertook more swimming training at Rugby, where the whole family had joined the club. Dad also gave me regular driving lessons.

At Leamington, I slotted into the team's starting lineup quickly alongside two current international players and a goalkeeper in the GB Under 20s. It was good to be playing at a higher level, and I knew I could improve and kick on.

Dad suggested I take a few proper driving lessons once I had finished my exams and moved permanently to Rugby before going off to college. He would pay for two or three for my upcoming eighteenth birthday if I sorted out the rest. So the plan was that I could hopefully drive by the end of the summer and get hold of a vehicle before heading off to college.

Back in Halesowen, my eighteenth came around on a less-than-inspiring regular school Monday. I had a few cards in the post at Mrs Rea's, but that was about it. Back then, an eighteenth birthday did not represent a 'coming of age', when a person effectively and legally became an adult - that time was still three years off.

The only thing that opened up for me was the ability to buy a pint legally in a pub. As this was something that I had been doing for a couple of years already, it was no big deal. So that evening, I had a couple of desultory beers with Derek and a few other friends straight after school. After that, I took the bus back up Mucklow Hill to see what culinary delights Mrs Rea had magically produced for my tea.

The date, however, told me I was in my last couple of months of school. It would also be just a short period of living in Halesowen before becoming an itinerant student.

That Whit holiday, we went to Wales as usual, and I could pick up my relationship with my lovely Welsh girlfriend Ruth.

I had brought some revision notes with me, but spending my time with her seemed much more preferable than studying. Honestly, the complete process was boring for me. I felt the last year had been all about preparing for the 'A' levels, going over examination techniques, having facts rammed home and constantly revisiting topics. It was undoubtedly not about opening up any new horizons – this was particularly the case with geography. So, it was pretty easy to skip the revision and head off with Ruth to check out the charming New Quay pubs.

Wider afield in the spring and summer of 1967, a social revolution was taking place in the USA. The Vietnam War was certainly not going well for the wealthiest and most powerful nation on the planet. The war had been rumbling on for many years. There was increasingly growing discontent about the massive human and military costs of conducting what many considered an unwinnable war on the far side of the world. Anti-war demonstrations were breaking out all over the USA, and there was considerable campus unrest in many colleges. Protesters were burning their draft cards, and they stripped Mohammed Ali, the former Cassius Clay, of his World heavyweight title for refusing the draft. They were calling up kids my age to fight and die in some distant oriental lands for unfathomable reasons.

In San Francisco, a counter-revolution was taking place against a backdrop of music from Jefferson Airplane, the

Grateful Dead, and The Byrds. Beat poet Timothy Leary encouraged people to 'turn on, tune in, and drop out'. The district of Haight Ashbury in the city was becoming the epicentre for an anti-war, anti-establishment, anti-racism hippie movement. They countenanced 'letting it all hang out'. They lived in squats, took psychedelic drugs and listened to West Coast rock.

Throughout the country, particularly in the south, as the long steamy summer took hold, violent race riots broke out in many places, and the Black Power movement gained strength. By the end of the period, they had recorded that some one hundred and fifty separate riots had taken place.

We in the UK observed the social and political unrest from a distance, understanding and abhorring the massive loss of lives on both sides in Vietnam. On the news, we saw the effect of the devastating carpet bombing of Laos and the use of brutal deforestation chemicals like Agent Orange in the jungles of Vietnam.

They sprayed twenty million gallons of the abominable stuff over countless acreages. The defoliation compounds caused the immediate death and suffering of some three million people and cruelly affected the lives of millions as yet unborn. The appalling chemicals caused a range of congenital disabilities and incidences of cancers and other life-threatening diseases.

For people of our age on the cusp of adulthood, we could certainly empathise with the students on the American campuses. They were living with the threat of being drafted to go to Indo-China *'to go and kill the yellow man,'* as Springsteen was later to put it. Why?

We also certainly had racial tensions, discrimination, and rioting in the UK throughout my time in the West Midlands. I remember, somewhere close to home, Smethwick, where I swam regularly, electing a Tory MP in 1964 who fought the election on the slogan

"If you want a nigger for a neighbour, vote Liberal or Labour."

Quite incendiary.

However, the level of hatred, prejudice and violence seen that summer in the States was totally beyond that league.

As eighteen-year-olds about to leave school and go on to employment or further education, while having sober, thoughtful and quite earnest discussions about Vietnam and the troubling racial situation throughout America, we gravitated more towards the counter-culture coming out of California. We could embrace that philosophy in an increasingly hirsute manner –'peace and love, man.'

Scott Mackenzie's 'Let's Go to San Francisco,' written by John Phillips of the Mamas and the Papas fame, became the anthem of the 'Summer of Love'. The vibe from that west coast city was to embrace free love (the birth control pill now being ubiquitous was most helpful in that regard), communal living, psychedelic drugs (I, for one, stuck to beer), anti-capitalism and joyous music. Tune in and drop out indeed - and don't forget to wear some flowers in your hair.

The Beatles released the brilliant Sergeant Pepper album in May, and I bought it straight away. Sergeant Pepper was the musical backdrop that summer and brilliant offerings from the Stones, the Who, and the Doors. The Clapton-led 'supergroup' Cream also commanded my attention along with 'Purple Haze' by Hendrix and the fabulous 'Whiter Shade of Pale' by Procol Harum.

It was all Carnaby Street, Mary Quant, Twiggy, mini-skirts and free love in the tabloids. In Birmingham, as well as in the capital, youth culture and the local music scene were vibrant and exciting. Sober column inches in the broadsheets focussed on a generation gap and the lowering of social standards, these arguments being offered as a counterpoint to the hippy philosophy.

I had grown my hair reasonably long (it had to be practical for swimming) and cultivated my sideburns. Mum and Dad did not approve, but I was not living with them. They seemed to be quite disbelieving about the astonishing speed with which so much was changing.

Early June got "A" levels out of the way. I did minimal revision (reading through notes the evening before and then cramming in some last-minute stuff at the crack of dawn). Still, I came out of the examination hall each time I sat a paper, thinking that while I would probably not be setting the world on fire, I would have no problem achieving my aim of getting into Loughborough. I was in a lucky position, but others of my contemporaries were sweating blood.

I hung around for a week after I had finished my final exam, waiting until my mates had similarly completed their efforts. We then embarked on a bacchanalian few days of celebration in pubs and at house parties. Finally, I said my goodbyes to friends and Mrs Rea and hitched off to Rugby.

CHAPTER 15

THE SUMMER OF LOVE

Dad's chatting to the taciturn and often cantankerous Bath's Superintendent, Mr Dick, had paid dividends, and he had set me up with a job at the outdoor pool.

They had constructed the pool, some seventy metres long, about fifteen across, and with a fountain at one end, way back in pre-war days. It was in the valley of the River Avon on the outskirts of town. Benefitting from extensive lawns, it was popular with picnicking families in the summer when the weather was warm and sunny. It was a well-regarded community asset.

Wooden changing chalets flanked both sides on the site's edges, and there was a combined ticket office and basket store at the entrance. (Swimmers placed clothes in wire baskets that were handed out on arrival and then taken to the basket store for safekeeping.) Opposite the turnstiles was a basic ancient plant room where the dour Scot, Mr Dick, gave me a no-frills crash course in swimming pool technical management. He showed me how to undertake water tests, record the results, and top up the alum tank (aluminium sulphate). This was to keep the water in tip-top sparkling condition. Old man Dick also showed me how to change the chlorine bottles when they were empty. The 'backwash' procedure to reverse the water flow in the filters and effectively clean out the accumulated debris from the latter was also a key part of my training.

With just an hour of Mr Dick's instructions and exhortations delivered in his succinct Aberdonian burr, I felt I had a complete grasp of the requirements. He put in a couple of early appearances to watch me undertake a backwash. Giving the plant room the once over, to see it was spick and span, he judged me to be competent on both counts with a couple of grunts.

"Fine. Fine. You've got this lad."

From the terse and often monosyllabic Scot, I took this to be a ringing endorsement of my all-around skills as a swimming pool engineer.

Satisfied that his precious swimming pool plant was in reasonably capable hands, he then toddled back up to Regent Street and left us in peace for a week or two.

The pool did not open until the school holidays started in July, so we had to get the place shipshape for a few weeks in June and early July. It was just two ladies who had regularly worked at the lido previously and me. Over several days, we weeded the broad area of paving slabs that had accumulated substantial grass growth and a profusion of dandelions since the previous September. Other jobs included tidying up the basket rooms and giving them a lick of paint. We also thoroughly scrubbed and disinfected the wooden changing cabins and the duckboards that were placed on the bare concrete floor.

Most of the time, the weather was quite glorious, so working out in the sunshine weeding or cleaning was not exactly onerous. I would work away at a steady pace, in shorts and stripped to the waist. I was developing an excellent early-season tan. Also, along with my increasingly long hair and sideburns, I was turning into some form of a quasi-hippy-beach bum.

"Your coffee is ready, John."

This would be a regular call from one of the women, Mary, an attractive, slim, blonde woman of about thirty, who looked out for me. I would then take a relaxing coffee break and put my feet up for a while.

To be honest, being a pool attendant and general factotum here was quite a doddle. Before long, we had all virtually worked ourselves out of a job with quite a few days remaining before we were open to the public. In the end, with all the tasks undertaken, I would just sit in the sun with a book getting through a suggested list of suitable novels provided by Loughborough. *Catcher in the Rye*, *To Kill a Mockingbird*, and *There Must Be a Pony* stick out in my memory.

I would also perhaps do a few lengths of the pool and behave as if I were on holiday. If old man Dick put in a rare appearance, we would go on a tour of inspection, and I could satisfy him that everything was tickety-boo.

If the weather was wet, as it was only rarely, we would sit in the office, play cards, and drink coffee. The ladies taught me a whole range of new card games.

Eventually, some additional staff joined us, and we could let in paying customers. Mr Dick expected us to be at work at 9 am, even though we did not open until 10.30 am. Because I was on top of everything, this meant I had the best part of an hour every day sunbathing, reading, drinking coffee or playing cards before the public came in. It was an excellent job.

At the other end of the day, we closed at 8 pm, but it was inevitably quiet towards the end of the proceedings so that I could always leave bang on time.

Being only a couple of miles from home, I rode to work on an old bike of my brother's. Going home nightly, a Grimsby fish lorry, on his regular route, would overtake me as I laboured up the hill. Belching out diesel fumes mixed with an all-pervasive stench of fish, it was not pleasant. Just as I was trying to suck in all the air I needed to get me up the incline, this was not something I needed. A bugger that.

One day in August, the postman gave me a letter just as I left for work, so I stuffed it in my pocket and headed off. Once settled with my first coffee of the day, I opened the envelope to reveal my results. Not the predicted As and Cs, but completely acceptable Bs and Ds. Four decent A-level passes. I was going to Loughborough.

The results were those I expected, but it relieved me massively that the letter confirmed my immediate short-term future.

The next important thing on my agenda was sorting out a driving test and getting hold of some cheap second-hand wheels. My work commitments made slotting in lessons tricky, but I scheduled four or five intensive sessions. I had an outstanding teacher, an avuncular and very helpful recently retired police officer.

After the last session with him, he declared me ready for the test and duly booked me up. It was quite a straightforward process in those days. Dad had given me a decent grounding when I first came back to Rugby, so the ex-copper just had to polish up my road skills and focus on exam techniques.

After some intensive revision, I knew the Highway Code thoroughly and sailed through the questions; then, it was time for the actual physical test. I was in the mini, which I had become used to and enjoyed driving. I was self-critical of my 'reversing around a corner' effort, which was not great. But the test went OK. The result was that the examiner handed me a pink slip to show I had passed.

As they held the driving tests close to the main post office, I drove straight round to Dad's place of employment. I parked up and then coincidentally saw Dad in conversation with Paul, his former employee from Cheadle, whom he had encouraged to join him at Rugby. They were standing in the car park.

My instructor stayed in the car whilst I walked over to tell them the news.

"I passed, Dad!"

At that moment, I saw Dad look at Paul with a raised eyebrow. I think Dad saw I had noticed the gesture.

The exchange hurt me, and I believe he was thinking,

"Yeah. I knew you would. Golden Balls has done it again!"

"Anyway, got to get back now. See you later," I quickly interjected and headed off.

I think he had concerns about my brothers, who had a few bullying and settling-in issues at school. These were matters I was not completely aware of. Somehow, however, I had sailed through life relatively serenely to date. This appeared to bug him a little. My year at Mrs Rea's had made me more independent, but this brief exchange strengthened my resolve to be increasingly self-contained in the future.

The incident cut me. Why could Dad not be pleased for me? Perhaps he was, but did not want to show it. To me it appeared he had cut me adrift – he could not waste any time with me when he had more pressing issues to resolve with my younger siblings.

Yes, I determined I would be even more autonomous and self-reliant in the future.

That said, I still intended to go on our summer holiday as part of the family group. I had cleared with Mr Dick at the start of my employment that I would like to have time off in August. We would be off as a family for our annual break. This time for a change, we were off to Cornwall, to the beautiful, small but perfectly formed, Treyarnon Bay, just south of Padstow.

We were camping in a farmer's field, which he had just about turned into a basic campsite. The location was ideal, just a couple of hundred yards down a narrow lane from the wide arc of soft yellow sand of Treyarnon Bay. Facing due west, the gorgeous white-flecked Atlantic rollers came crashing up the beach in a smooth regular formation. Marram grass-covered dunes backed the wide sandy beach.

It was a fabulous beach for surfing, beach cricket, rock climbing and crabbing. We all had basic plywood bodyboards, and we were out in the ocean for hours at a time.

We explored the rock-fringed extremities of the beach at low tide, catching crabs. Or else swimming and snorkelling in a large, 30-yard-long six-foot-deep natural pool in the rocks, left behind by the receding tide.

There would also be mass games of cricket involving half the people on the beach. People always seemed to gravitate to our games, and it was a case of the more, the merrier, Dad to the forefront in getting things organised.

The Council employed Australian lifeguards to keep their eye on things and ensure people were bathing and boarding between the flags and keeping safe. Cornish beaches can be dangerous places.

One of these bronzed, fit young men, nicknamed Ajax, would send one or other of my brothers to Kelly's ice-cream van always parked up at the beach entrance. The code was 'Ajax sent me.'

And this would result in extra-large free ice creams all around – quite a bonus. It seemed to be acceptable behaviour. Maybe Kelly was trading well enough to handle a few freebies.

I had never seen Malibu board surfing before. However, I quickly appreciated the skills shown by a couple of off-duty Antipodeans and some adventurous locals. They were always out at the break-point beyond the surf, sat on their seven-foot-long fibreglass boards waiting for the next ride. Somewhat more exotic than our four-foot marine ply efforts with little curved ends. They rode the waves expertly into the shore, and it was brilliant to watch – and something I wanted to try at some stage.

In the early evening, with Mum and Dad preparing the evening meal, we would go down the lane to where one of the young locals, a lad of around fifteen, was brushing up on his surfing skills. He was using a small board that he had shaped and fixed onto a roller skate. He would ride down the slope with this basic gadget as if he was coming in on a wave.

This lad's name turned out to be Tigger Newlyn, who, a year or two later, became Britain's champion surfer and established a thriving business fabricating customised boards. His younger brother also became a pro surfer and went out to Australia to ply his trade.

My brothers became friendly with Tigger, and he generously let them go on his basic roller skateboard. They became reasonably proficient after a time and were keen to practise as much as possible. Being cool and eighteen years old, I decided it was inappropriate to have a go on what I deemed to be a child's toy.

I enjoyed watching, though, and thought it to be a brilliant concept. On returning to Rugby, my brothers built their versions of a skateboard. They were regularly flying down the steep slope of our road down to Shakespeare Gardens at the bottom, sometimes disastrously crashing as they rounded the tight bend.

I wish I could have seen the commercial potential in Tigger's design. It was 1967, but five years later, at Christmas 1972, the number one present for kids in the country was skateboards. They sold hundreds of thousands – such a chance missed.

To be fair, they had been around in California before 1967, so Tigger was probably not the inventor of the concept, but he was very much a pioneer.

In 2021, they even introduced skateboarding to great acclaim as a new Olympic sport in Tokyo.

I had told a few mates back in Halesowen I was going to Cornwall in the summer with my folks before I left. Four of them said they would come down and camp for a week with me. So for our second week, I took my little blue ridge tent off from the top field where Mum and Dad had set up their large, newly acquired continental frame tent. I went down to the lower area by the entrance, where the lads later joined me.

Dad had some doubts about a group of post 'A' level boys camping together, the potential hassle we could cause and the mischief to which we might get up. We behaved pretty well, though, not causing him any headaches or embarrassment as far as I recall.

We went out to Newquay one day, I remember, probably by a local bus. After swimming and surfing in the sea all day, together with a bit of sunbathing, we got ready for the evening. Naturally, we embarked on an extensive full-on pub and club crawl throughout the resort.

The small town was rapidly becoming a major hedonistic attraction to would-be hippies, surfers and music fans, and was buzzing with activity. All enjoyed a fun and good-natured evening, although there was a certain degree of happy inebriation. When the bars finally shut at around 2 am, we had no alternative but to walk the coast road back to Treyarnon. The walk was some thirteen miles but the way we were lurching across the highway in the dark, just a faint moon illuminating our path, we probably covered double that.

Through Porth, past Watergate Bay and Bedruthan, we meandered through the night. Up and down between bays and clifftops, we continued. Reaching our tents at dawn, we crashed out for the rest of the day. We were living the dream in the summer of love.

Back home after a great two weeks in Cornwall, I went back to the pool to work until the schools went back in early September.

At around this time, I was on the lookout for a car. I needed something that would enable me to get to Leamington and back regularly, travel the forty-odd miles to Loughborough and allow me to be in control of my destiny. I looked through the local paper and, with Dad's help, chose an old Ford Anglia going for thirty quid. We knocked the guy selling it privately down to twenty-seven pounds ten, but I still think he had the better part of the deal. Mechanically, it was sound, but there was evidence of some less-than-professional bodywork repairs, and I would soon require two replacement tyres. Still, it got me mobile. I soon learned that running a car with all the associated fuel, tax, insurance, and maintenance costs was a considerable drain on financial resources.

When we closed up the pool for the season, I was planning to go off on another adventure. I was looking forward to my first-ever trip to Europe. I had arranged with another friend from school, Merv, actually to go abroad, camping. Something I had never done in my life and very much wanted to.

I had plenty of time before going up to Loughborough at the end of September, and Merv had even longer before he started his university course. The plan was to go hitchhiking through France for a couple of weeks.

There was no particular strategy in mind. We would make it up as we went along and see where the lifts took us. Unfortunately, annoyingly and frustratingly, Merv dropped out last minute. Still, I decided I would go through with the trip. I, therefore, prepared for my first excursion abroad being a solo venture.

The date soon came around, and I was ready for the off with my rucksack packed, sleeping bag and tent on the top. I had stashed my new passport safely in my anorak pocket.

It was not a good hitchhiking day. I had left later than I had wanted to because I had a few tasks to attend to in the morning. However, I felt I would have sufficient time to get down to Southampton by nightfall. I was aiming to catch a ferry to Le Havre, Cherbourg or Caen. Stranded on the roadside for hours, I finally ended up thumbing on the main road in the middle of Newbury in the dark.

A quick decision meant aborting any ideas of getting any further that night. So I pitched my tent virtually where I was on a large roundabout on the A34. Heading off to a welcoming-looking pub, I had spotted for a pint and a pork pie for my supper.

I awoke at dawn and quickly struck camp. With a change of fortunes, I immediately got a lift with a truck going down to Southampton docks.

I took a ferry across to Le Havre and persuaded a truck driver to give me a lift out of the dreary and scruffy port. He took me to the main road heading towards the southwest. It was murky, grey, and a little cold, so I intended to get down to warmer latitudes as quickly as possible.

Hitching was a bit of a hit-and-miss day, but I got some miles under my belt, taking in Lisieux with its vast and spectacular Basilica, where I stopped for a coffee and croissant, as was the gallic tradition.

Travelling on to Alencon and Le Mans, heading ever southwards, it was most enjoyable watching the changing landscape slip by and observing the temperatures soar. Sunny and warm by now. This was more like it.

It was exciting to be speeding down a smooth tarmac road just outside Le Mans when we crossed under the famous Dunlop bridge, arching over the highway like a giant half-tyre. I only realised then that I had seen the scene on television and we were on a part of the famous 24-hour road circuit, which I was unaware used public roads.

Even though I had to wait for a while for lifts occasionally, it was ok. The weather was balmy, so it was not too disagreeable sitting on a grassy verge, enjoying the summer warmth. Listening to the busy buzzing of scores of insects, and watching the gaily coloured butterflies fluttering in the hedgerows or adjacent poppy-flecked cornfields was most acceptable.

I also found it fascinating to pick up some food for lunch. Stopping at an attractive village or small town, I could soon assemble a veritable picnic feast, visiting separate specialist shops. It amazed me that although I was only a couple of hundred miles from home, everything was just so different here.

I loved the large shiny red tomatoes that were sold readily at the greengrocers. I would go to a boulangerie and buy a freshly baked baguette. Then the charcuterie for some home-baked ham or pate and perhaps a patisserie for a beautiful fruit tart for my dessert.

The pace of life seemed so slow in rural France. Shopkeepers and customers had time for each other and were happy to have a polite chat. I also found, on future travel days occasionally and frustratingly, that if I was a little late in trying to buy my food, shopkeepers had rattled down their shutters for a couple of hours of lunch break.

I had failed my French 'O' level exam, but I had picked up a reasonable vocabulary. Verb endings were not my strength, but I got by just mumbling the final syllables of tricky verbs. I got by remarkably well.

At the end of a long day on the road, I would seek a campsite. I found small towns operated inexpensive municipal sites, which proved perfectly adequate. A small pitch and a decent shower block were my simple requirements.

Some sites were top-notch and in pretty places on the edge of town. I remember staying at one particular site in Châtellerault, perfectly sited close to the River Vienne in a wonderfully tranquil setting, but only a short walk into the delightful town.

My French came on well out of necessity. I needed to eat, drink and ask for directions in the native tongue, as English speaking in the French countryside seemed a bit of a no-no.

The experience of being in a different country — the language, the currency, the customs, and the architecture was all very new to me, and I found it all quite fascinating.

I stopped "pour une grande tasse de café au lait s'il vous plaît" at a town centre café somewhere on my journey one day. It intrigued me to see a group of three old chaps at the bar adding water to the liquor in their glasses, which changed the liquid to a milky yellowy-white. I investigated further and discovered the drink was pastis, an aniseed-flavoured liqueur. Liking the taste of aniseed, I ordered one up, added the water and joined the white-haired, ruddy-cheeked group of pensioners in conversation. We had no problems understanding each other, and we quickly developed our particular version of an entente cordiale.

Others came and went into the café. Several rapidly downed tiny little glasses of white wine or espresso coffees and were quickly on their way. Others morosely ordered a small beer and lit up a strong but not unpleasantly smelling Gauloises or Gitane. They would then sit poring over the day's edition of L'Equipe, the excellent daily sports newspaper.

Everything was polite and highly civilised, with "Bonjour monsieurs, bonjour madames" and "ca vas?" ringing out regularly. I loved the atmosphere of these little café-bars, such a wonderful ambience and so different from British pubs.

My route down vaguely towards the Atlantic coast brought me close to Angers. It was getting a little late in the day when an agreeable man of probably around thirty-five stopped for me, driving a smart new Citroen. We were some forty kilometres from the city. He was very chatty, interested in my journey and asked where I was aiming for, and I told him. He said Angers was quite a sizeable city, and he lived on this side of town. To reach the southern periphery this evening would be a little tricky, he said. After a bit of thought, he suggested I stay with him and his wife. He would then take me out to the outskirts the following day to continue my travels.

It seemed to be a perfect solution for me, as I was tired and hungry from a day's travelling. And soon, we were parking on the drive of an attractive modern detached house in the suburbs. His pretty dark-haired wife welcomed us, taking in her stride the fact that an English student was dropping in for supper unannounced. She immediately brought us both a beer as we made ourselves comfortable in their front room, while she returned and busied herself in the kitchen.

She brought us regular beer supplies as she updated us on the meal's progress. A call then came that dinner was about to be served and could we take our places at the table.

Dinner was very French with pate and bread, a casserole of pork with green beans and potatoes and tarte aux pommes and cheese to follow. We also had bountiful amounts of excellent red wine as we chatted. They seemed genuinely interested in my impressions of France, particularly on hearing that it was my first visit. They also asked me about England, my schooling, my family and my future ambitions.

With the meal finished and feeling very replete, (at least I was) Jerome and I retired to the sofa with a cognac and a coffee. Christiana did the clearing up. I did offer to help, but she waved me away.

Jerome suggested that if I was going to the coast around La Rochelle or Rochfort, I should visit one of the islands just offshore. These are now joined to the mainland by bridges. Many Parisians favoured the Ile d'Oleron and the more northerly Ile de Re for their holidays. They both boasted a vast array of glorious beaches, pretty little villages, and abundant seafood restaurants. Including ones for people with modest budgets, he added pointedly. I said I would certainly try to check them out.

Around 11.30 pm, feeling tired and probably a little fuzzy from the alcohol, I said I would like to retire. Thanking them for a lovely meal in my best French, I sauntered over to the stairs.

Christiana showed me up to my room, a perfectly sizeable double en suite room, and left me to it. The bed looked very inviting.

First, however, I went to the stylish bathroom to undertake my ablutions and tried out what I understood to be a bidet. I sat down, turned a tap and immediately let out a piercing scream as a powerful jet of red hot water shot up my anal orifice. My panicked shriek brought Christiana bounding up the stairs and knocking on my door to check I was alright. Embarrassed, I assured her I was fine, just a miscalculation, and I eventually got myself into bed. I have never been near a bidet since.

I slept well after my boiling water enema and went down for breakfast. After some fresh baguette, preserves, and several coffees, Jerome announced he would take me out to the far side of Angers, where I could hitchhike towards the south and west.

I thanked them both very much for their kindnesses and received a Gallic shrug from Jerome and,

"Pas de probleme!"

I think they were both quite amused at a young Englishman hitchhiking through France on his own and were pleased to help.

Over the next couple of days, I reached la Rochelle and, heeding Jerome's words, carried on to Ile d'Oleron.

A long modern bridge from the mainland linked us to the island's flattish landmass. Apparently, the causeway had only opened the previous year, and I presumed access would have been by the ferry before, so this was a lot more convenient. Ile d'Oleron measures a modest 30km by 8km but is the most significant French island on the Atlantic coast. It is also considerably bigger than the largest of the Channel Islands, Jersey.

Travelling in a battered old pickup truck, the rotund, nut-brown local dropped me at a crossroads on the main road. He showed me with a wave of the arm the way I should go. I had said I wanted a campsite close to a beach, and he was confident of where he was sending me. Nodding vigorously and grunting, "oui, oui, c'est bon" and "seulement deux kilometres". I thanked him, bade him farewell, and headed off.

It was delightfully warm and bright, and the bees, butterflies and birds were out in force in the hedgerows, making a wonderful soundtrack to my progress. It was a most enjoyable walk, passing neat little whitewashed houses with pretty flower-filled gardens, some with fishing nets drying on their garden walls.

The campsite was right next to the beach, and I found it quickly. I was on the island's west coast, and I could see the Atlantic rollers crashing up the wide sandy beach in regular formation. Tumbling over greeny-blue initially and then breaking into glorious bright white. This would be an ideal place to stay for a while.

The coastline, which was backed by extensive sections of dark green pine forests, looked terrific to me. After I had booked in and erected my little two-man tent, I took a walk. Unencumbered by my hefty rucksack and just wearing shorts and flip-flops, I strolled along in a carefree manner, appreciating the strong sunshine on my back.

It was simply magnificent for a Brit on his first trip abroad to be under the cloudless blue sky. A giant golden sun was so gloriously warming, unlike the low-wattage version found shining down on the Lincolnshire beaches of my early days. It was also, as I found a little later, a place to appreciate truly spectacular crimson sunsets from my perch at a simple little beach bar.

By the time I had gone back to base and sorted out some much-needed washing in the camp laundry, it was late afternoon. So I relaxed with a beer at the aforementioned bar. I intended to stay for a few days now. I had found my paradise, and I would have plenty of time to enjoy the beach and the sea.

The sun, a beach, a decent campsite and a welcoming bar. What more could I wish for?

The bar offered a simple bread and seafood soup meal. This was more than satisfactory for my evening repast, and not long after the sun had dipped below the horizon, I retired for the night.

I woke early the next day, listening to the waves and the seagulls, and went straight down to the beach after a coffee at the snack bar on site. I had to go for a swim. It amazed me when I braced myself for the chill on my toes on entering the surf to find that the water was swimming pool temperature. It was a pleasure to just walk into waist depth and then dive through the incoming breakers without shivering from the cold.

I swam out beyond the breakers to the flatter water and completed a couple of hundred yards, pulling and kicking vigorously. The physical effort of swimming was enjoyable.

I then came inshore a little to where the waves were breaking to do some body surfing. The sizeable waves regularly carried me breathlessly on long rides into the shallows. I decided there was no need for me to get a surfboard because body surfing was the way to go.

Finally, muscles aching pleasingly, I walked out of the foamy shallows. For the first time in my life, I experienced coming out of the sea and being warm. A balmy breeze washed over me, drying my skin swiftly and allowing me to feel the heat of the sun on my back and legs. I sauntered up the beach, embracing this unfamiliar feeling. The experience was otherworldly compared to emerging from the cold grey North Sea at Skeggy. Since Chapel St. Leonards, I had experienced warm sunny days in Wales or Cornwall on our family holidays, but nothing compared to this.

I spent four or five days on the island, enjoying the beach all day. Grabbing a filled baguette for lunch, I would then go for long exploratory walks in the evenings. It was simple to find modest little bars and restaurants for my evening meal.

One evening I pushed the boat out and went to somewhere a little more upmarket for my dinner and chose a huge seafood platter. *"Un plateau de fruits de mer"*, according to the menu, which seemed popular with other diners. Rather like a cake stand produced for afternoon tea at posh hotels, they brought a sizeable tiered plate out overflowing with cascading crustacea sitting on a bed of ice. There was a dressed crab, mussels, clams, oysters, langoustines, crevettes, king prawns and other unrecognisable offerings from the deep. The immaculately attired waiter brought something like nutcrackers, a sizeable finger bowl, a side salad, bread, butter, aioli and other accompaniments.

I dived into this culinary experience with some enthusiasm, having eaten only modestly all day. Sipping my Muscadet sur lie (a favourite of mine to this day) I thought it was all rather marvellous. Although I was a little perturbed when I approached some indeterminate creature from the deep on the edge of the platter. It stuck out an impertinent pseudopodium towards me, as if to say,

Don't eat me, mate.

I decided the creature was right, and I left him untouched on the plate. The rest of the meal, though, was delicious.

Reluctantly, a few days later, I had to leave my temporary island home and head back north to one of the channel ports and back to England.

Hitching was again a bit hit-and-miss. In the UK it was reasonably straightforward thumbing a ride, but the French probably felt somewhat differently about the practice.

One day, I had been waiting at the roadside for about an hour with no joy. Suddenly an archetypical French man, moustachioed and wearing a black beret, Gitane hanging from his bottom lip and a baguette strapped to the back pannier, passed me on his motorised bicycle. These were quite common in rural France, seemingly ordinary bikes but with a small petrol engine mounted on the front allowing them to travel at up to 15mph. I was becoming so desperate for a lift that I contemplated purchasing such a vehicle and even tried to see whether I could buy one in the next town when I finally got there.

It was a rather silly idea, which I rapidly abandoned, becoming more philosophical about the difficulties of hitchhiking and deciding to take the rough with the smooth.

I treated myself one evening on my circuitous route back up north, dining at quite an elegant hotel restaurant and enjoying an excellent succulent steak with frites and salad. Whilst tucking into my meal, I noticed a couple who had been sitting in the corner finish their meal and head out of the dining room. They had left a good half bottle of red wine, and I thought, *"What a waste, I might as well have that."*

I sidled across to snaffle it before the waiter cleared the bottle away.

"Non, Monsieur. Non!"

A waiter admonished me on his return to the room.

He had seen what had happened and tried to explain that the guests were staying at the hotel and would finish the wine the following evening.

A little embarrassing, but *c'est la vie,* I thought. Win a few, lose a few.

I was enjoying my first foreign travel adventure a lot, though; it opened my eyes to experience a different culture, language and dialects, cuisine and climate. It set in motion a lifelong wanderlust and a desire to see and experience more and more of the world. I knew from this briefest of forays that more foreign journeys would be on the cards for me in the future.

I also learned to keep my wits about one when travelling. A young couple in their thirties picked me up, who said they could drop me in Le Havre. This was as I neared the end of my trip and was just about to take the ferry home.

Initially, they seemed friendly enough, and the woman would turn around smilingly to chat and ask about my trip, but there was also a bit of furtive whispering between the couple. I had some suspicions as they discussed where they could best drop me off as we crossed the impressive Pont de Tancarville over the Seine.

I twigged something was going on. They seemed to be a little disingenuous when they stopped. They encouraged me to get out first and go round to the other side of the vehicle to retrieve my rucksack from the opposite door. I resisted this option as a sixth sense told me not to leave my bag as I was sure the intention was just to whizz off with my possessions. A load of grubby clothing, an ancient tent and a well-used sleeping bag would not represent much of a haul, but obviously not something I wanted to happen. I foiled the plan and could see that it disappointed them not to have pulled off the stunt as I thanked them for the lift and said goodbye. The man particularly did not look at all impressed.

I later enjoyed an indulgent last meal of the holiday in the sophisticated restaurant onboard the ferry to round off the trip. As I relaxed with brandy, the English Channel slipped by through the large picture windows. I took stock, swirling the amber fluid around the balloon glass in a contemplative manner.

A new phase of my life was about to begin. For a few years, I was going to become a full-time student. Reflecting on my journey through life to date, I considered how things might pan out in the future.

It had been quite a journey from my conception (allegedly) on a windblown sand hill just outside Skegness to where I was today. Now a young adult, I was on the cusp of enjoying new and life-enhancing experiences. Being a PE student was something I had relished doing for many years. I would embrace the opportunity and put all my efforts into studying, improving my sporting performance, making friends, and being positive about what life would throw at me.

I did not know exactly what the future held. But I was certain there would be many experiences to enjoy, many additional aspects of life to appreciate, and friendships to build and maintain. This was something that had eluded me to date because of being constantly shuffled around the country and regularly moving schools. I had lost touch with earlier friends. I appreciated the importance of camaraderie and by now realised nurturing such relationships was something that needed working on.

While enjoying the company of like-minded people, I was also quite self-reliant. I think I had always been quite independent. When Merv had dropped out of this trip, there was no question of me not continuing with the plans. I was very glad I had done so. My first visit to the continent had certainly whetted my appetite for foreign travel. It was something I wanted to undertake more frequently, with company or perhaps even alone.

I reflected on my happy childhood. My parents had always done their best for me and my siblings. I understood Dad's ambition and that his overriding consideration was to do well for his family in striving for his various promotions. While I had sailed through life and took whatever challenges were thrown up, I know the changes had affected my brothers somewhat.

Dad had pre-empted my concerns about having to move to Rugby for the final year of my schooling. The answer, farming me out to Mrs Rea suited everyone. For me, I was glad about the early autonomy. At seventeen, I was already living the life of a student, without parents breathing down my neck or trying to change my behaviour. I enjoyed having Mrs Rea as my landlady. We had a good working relationship, and I appreciated being able to come and go as I pleased and being treated as an adult. For Mum and Dad, I felt they thought it was quite appropriate for me to fly the nest and they could concentrate their efforts on helping my brothers through adolescence.

Over my eighteen years, I had seen so many changes in society. I was born in the late forties and grew up in the utilitarian fifties. This was a period when the country was very much finding its feet after the devastating impact of World War 2. In my early years, I could remember food rationing and daily cod liver oil. For many families, refrigerators, motor cars, television sets and even telephones were not the norm. By scrimping and saving over a long period, perhaps they could buy these modern acquisitions, but they would not come readily. For the average person, flying off for sunny holidays was almost science fiction.

My teenage years were in the sixties, which was a decade when the country went through massive changes. I was just the right age to appreciate the growing youth culture and enjoy the revolution in popular music. It disconcerted adults that there was much comment about the 'generation gap.'

This current year, with the 'peace and love' vibe coming out of California, was already being dubbed the 'summer of love.' It was undoubtedly the perfect time to become a full-time student.

I was in a good place and was looking forward to the future. I was happy with life and thought I would reward myself with another snifter. The glass was half full.